Junior Year Abroad

Books By Rosamond du Jardin

Tobey Heydon Books

Practically Seventeen (1949)
Class Ring (1951)
Boy Trouble (1953)
The Real Thing (1956)
Wedding in the Family (1958)
One of the Crowd (1961)

Marcy Rhodes Books:

Wait for Marcy (1950)
Marcy Catches Up (1952)
A Man for Marcy (1954)
Senior Prom (1957)

Pam & Penny Howard Books:

Double Date (1951)
Double Feature (1953)
Showboat Summer (1955)
Double Wedding (1959)

Non-Series Titles

Someone to Count on (1962)
Young and Fair (1963)
Junior Year Abroad (1960)

Adult Novels

All is Not Gold (1935)
Only Love Lasts (1937)
Honorable Estate (1943)
Brief Glory (1944)
Tomorrow Will Be Fair (1946)

Junior Year Abroad

BY

ROSAMOND AND JUDY DU JARDIN

Image Cascade Publishing
www.ImageCascade.com

MANUFACTURED IN THE UNITED STATES
OF AMERICA

A hardcover edition of this book was originally published by J. B. Lippincott Company. It is here reprinted by arrangement with HarperCollins Publishers.

First *Image Cascade Publishing* edition published 2003.

Library of Congress Cataloging in Publication Data
Du Jardin, Rosamond
Du Jardin, Judy
Junior year abroad.

(Juvenile Girls)
Reprint. Originally published: New York & Philadelphia: J. B. Lippincott Company, 1960.

ISBN 1-930009-80-1 (Pbk.)

To Rusty and Steve
who helped live this story

FOREWORD

Ever since I began writing books for teen-agers, two questions have been asked over and over again in the large volume of fan mail I receive. Girls from all over the United States and even as far away as Japan have written to ask: "Are the characters in your stories real people?" And, "Did the things you write about ever actually happen to anyone you know?"

Always I have had to answer, "No, these are fictional characters." And while I might adapt an infrequent incident from real life for use in a story, the plots in general have been fictional, too.

But this is a different sort of book. All of the characters in it are real people, although some of their names have been changed. Every single incident related here really happened. Judy is my younger daughter and the letters she wrote home from France during her year's study there were so entertaining and filled with adventures, I thought teen-agers everywhere might enjoy them. And so, together, we have adapted them into a book. The story is entirely from Judy's viewpoint, in a great many parts it is in her own words. And I hope that girls who have enjoyed reading about Tobey, and Marcy and the twins, Pam and Penny, will enjoy Judy's story, too.

ROSAMOND DU JARDIN.

CONTENTS

1

THE ADVENTURE BEGINS

As Rusty and I climbed the gangplank of the large, but far from new ship that was to carry us to Europe, I suppose we looked quite calm to a detached observer. Just two tall slim girls, one blond and green-eyed, one auburn-haired with brown eyes, boarding a ship along with a great many other people, as though it were the most ordinary thing in the world. Maybe Rusty was calm, I reflected. I didn't know her well enough to be sure what was going on in her mind. But I was so excited, I was about to pop. And I kept thinking over and over, This is it, Judy. You're here and it's really happening. This is the beginning of the big adventure!

Only, of course, it wasn't the beginning at all.

The chain of events leading to this improbable moment had started a year and a half before in Mr. Wheeler's office. Mr. Wheeler was my faculty advisor at Park College and my sociology professor as well. And since sociology was my major, his opinion carried a good deal of weight with me. He had asked me that day to be his assistant the following year. And I had leaped at the chance. We had sat for a time discussing my future duties, which sounded fascinating. Then locking his hands behind his head, my advisor asked thoughtfully, "And after next year, do you know what I think you should do?"

I could only stare dumbly, having no idea of what he might be getting at.

"You're intelligent," he went on and, although I certainly didn't feel so at the moment, I appreciated the compliment. "You're good at languages and your interests are broad, especially in people and their problems. Moreover, you've said you want to write some day. And a writer needs a background of wide experience. In view of all that," his youthfully earnest glance impaled me like a butterfly on a pin, "I definitely think you should plan to spend your junior year abroad."

That had really been the beginning. For as soon as Mr. Wheeler made his suggestion, I saw at once what a wonderful thing it would be. My junior year abroad—why, I should have thought of it myself! The mere idea of studying in Europe made my imagination catch fire. France, Italy, Switzerland, Germany—the possibilities were endless and dazzling. And lots of girls were doing it. My parents shouldn't be too hard to persuade—I hoped!

I wrote home at once, broaching the subject as gently as possible. Even so, it had the effect of a bombshell on my mother and father. After all, I'm their youngest child and my sister and brother are married. My mother keeps busy writing books for teenagers and my father has a bookstore to occupy him. Still, they lavish a good deal of their time and attention on me. They had grown accustomed to having me in college a couple of states away from Illinois. But Europe! That was different.

However, they're reasonable people. And I had plenty of time to work on them. By fall they had agreed to the idea, at least to the extent of letting me go ahead and investigate various programs.

"If only," my mother commented wistfully, "Europe wasn't so far away that you can't even get home for Christmas!"

I knew darned well I'd miss them, too, away over there on the other side of the Atlantic. Ours is a close-knit clan, whose members enjoy each other's company. But this was too good a chance to miss. I just had to take advantage of it.

And so I began checking on foreign study plans, sorting and sifting and eliminating. I finally decided on the program offered by the Institute for American Universities, in Aix-en-Provence, France. This nonprofit private organization, according to its catalog, offered a new educational dimension to properly qualified students. It provided a center for direct and intensive study of European culture and civilization and had been planned especially to provide this service for American colleges.

Every aspect of this particular program appealed to me. France from the start had been my preference. Not only was I of French descent, but this was the foreign language I knew best. Instruction at the Institute was in English for students whose French was not adequate. On the other hand, the Institute was affiliated with the University of Aix-Marseilles and students who were fluent in French could study also at that centuries-old university. Instruction at the Institute was along the lines of the standard American curriculum, thus credits could be earned toward one's graduation from an American college. And the cost, including trans-Atlantic travel, was no more than at an average American school. All in all, the set-up sounded as nearly perfect as we could hope for. So I began making the necessary arrangements.

That was a busy and exciting fall. My work as assistant in the sociology department proved interesting, my classes stimulating. In my spare time I worked on the school paper. And, of course, I dated.

At first I dated several young men. It's always like that in September, unless you're pinned or engaged, which I wasn't. But as the leaves on the campus trees fell and winter drew on, the field narrowed sharply. I began to see more and more of a tall individual named Bradley Carlsen. Brad had very short dark hair, a nice grin, a direct blue glance through shell-rimmed glasses and a knack of worming his way into my thoughts and refusing to be dislodged no matter how hard I worked at it. After a while I gave up trying and just let him linger there in the edges of my consciousness most of the time.

Naturally we discussed in detail my spending the following year in Europe. One evening as we sat in the dorm lounge, with a stack of Brad's classical records making soft music in the background, he said, "You'll be gone from September till the middle of June." The way he said this, it sounded like several years.

"Yes," I sighed.

"Lots of things can happen in that length of time."

But not to us, to the wonderful way we were just beginning to feel about each other, I hoped. It was too soon yet to know if we were really falling in love. But

I was already so fond of him I didn't want it spoiled. Something deep within me ached at the very thought.

"If we last through ten months apart," I said, "and still feel this way—" It didn't seem necessary to go on.

"Yeah," Brad agreed, his big hand closing hard around mine.

He didn't try to dissuade me from going. After all, the machinery had been set in motion. My application had been accepted by the Institute, fees paid, my ship ticket ordered. Aside from all that, though, Brad felt as I did that this opportunity for study abroad was too wonderful for me to miss.

"I wish I could go over, too," he told me. But since he couldn't, he had no intention of standing in my way . . .

All during my sophomore year and the summer that followed, I saw a great deal of Brad. Our homes were hundreds of miles apart, but he managed to get a summer job in our area and spend all his free time at our house. This was sheer bliss, although it didn't make the prospect of our separation any easier. In fact, as my time of departure drew nearer, I didn't see how I was going to stand leaving him.

I thought some long serious thoughts during those sunny days and moonlit nights. Not only would I be parting from Brad, but from my family and all my old friends. I'd be turning my back, too, on the pleasant surroundings I knew and loved, in order to face new people, different experiences, a strange way of life in a foreign country. Sometimes I felt I'd been out of my mind even to consider such a thing. Then again, the future beckoned beguilingly.

It helped some when I got my first letter from Rusty. Her name was really Barbara Stanley and she had written to the Institute to find out if another girl from anywhere in her vicinity was going to Aix-en-Provence. Mr. Maza, who answered, apparently feeling we were neighbors, living in Iowa and Illinois, had given her my name and address. And so we began corresponding.

I strongly suspected, though, that we had very little in common. Rusty was a sorority girl, up to her eyebrows in sorority activities at the big University of Iowa. She was also one of the Highlanders, a well-known marching band unit that performed at football games. I, on the other hand, had chosen a small college and one that didn't sanction sororities or fraternities because I just wasn't keen on the whole idea of them. And while I enjoyed the social side of college life, it wasn't my main interest.

Still, even though we might not prove too congenial, I was glad to know in advance another student who would be attending the Institute. We could lend each other moral support in a strange land, I told myself. And soon, by letter, she and I had decided that it would be nice if her parents could bring her by car as far as my home near Chicago. Then the two of us could fly from there to New York and thence embark for Europe.

Looking back, it seemed that the summer had passed like one of those movie montages that scramble people and places and events all together to depict the passage of time. There was my passport to get. I had to be vaccinated. Also, there was the tremendous task of assembling my wardrobe. Mr. Maza had informed all prospective students that in French schools one did not wear ankle socks, slacks, Bermudas, or very bright colors. This necessitated some drastic changes in my usual school apparel. And in addition to shopping, there was the overwhelming job of packing. I was determined to get sufficient clothing and accessories for ten months into one wardrobe trunk, one large suitcase and a train case. And I succeeded, too, but it wasn't easy.

Our trunks had been sent ahead weeks ago; they should be safely stowed away by this time in the ship's hold. Our smaller luggage should be awaiting us in our cabins. And here we were, practically on our way, feeling under our feet for the first time in our lives the deck of an ocean liner.

"Isn't it exciting?" Rusty breathed, her warm brown eyes sparkling.

"I'm clutched!" I agreed. But the words came out a little husky through the enormous lump in my throat.

2

WE SAIL

We had boarded the ship around three-thirty in the afternoon, expecting to sail within the hour. Still, we figured we could take a quick look at our respective cabins before sailing time. Mine was on B deck, which might as well have stood for "bottom." It proved to be about ten feet by twenty-five and contained eight bunks. Closet space was so limited I could see myself living out of my suitcase the entire voyage. But I didn't mind too much, after the initial shock. One didn't expect luxury traveling tourist class on a ship predominantly filled with students. And besides, I reminded myself, I'd be spending very little time in my cabin.

Rusty and I met in the corridor of the deck above and I asked how her cabin was.

"Small," she admitted. "More crowded than you can even imagine."

I shook my head. "I don't have to imagine."

"Oh, well," Rusty's spectacular smile flashed, "we didn't expect the Queen Elizabeth."

"And after all," I smiled back, "we'll only be using our cabins to sleep in."

"Ah, sleep," Rusty sighed. "What's that?"

It was certainly something we hadn't got much of lately.

Rusty and her parents had arrived at our house in the evening three days ago. Some friends and members of our clan, my brother and his wife and her parents, were gathered for a farewell party. Only I wasn't feeling in a very partyish mood, since Brad had had to leave for home several days earlier. It had been hard to let him go. How was I going to exist for ten months without that man, I wondered?

The Stanleys' arrival proved a welcome diversion. Rusty's parents were charming, but the word seemed scarcely adequate to describe their daughter. Rusty was lovely in a striking way. Curly mahogany-red hair framed her animated face, with the warm sweet smile and beautifully expressive deep brown eyes. Hers was the type of attraction which immediately draws, like a magnet, every male in the vicinity, but without antagonizing all the females. Everyone at the party fell under Rusty's spell. You just couldn't help yourself. And, for the first time since he had gone, I felt glad Brad hadn't been able to stay any longer.

Our combined families saw us off for New York the following morning. As our mothers kissed us good-bye, their eyes were suspiciously bright, but no tears fell while we were near enough to see. We talked steadily during the three-hour flight and by the end of it we felt at least a little better acquainted. But I was still convinced we had very little in common. Rusty was more poised than I, more sure of herself. Her big-college-sorority background had given her an aura of sophistication and self-confidence I couldn't begin to match. But she didn't act at all superior or unpleasant about it.

When I told her that a boy I knew, now stationed at an air force base in New Hampshire, was going to look me up during our day and a half in New York before our ship sailed, Rusty obligingly offered to make herself scarce. But I assured her this wasn't necessary. Dave and I were simply old friends who had kept in touch by letter since my high school days.

"You're sure I won't be in the way?" Rusty pressed. "I can perfectly well go sight-seeing on my own."

She was completely sincere, but I wouldn't hear of it. So she and Dave and I went out to see the town together. During the rest of that afternoon and evening and most of the following day, we really hit the high spots. Rusty hadn't been in New York before, I'd seen it just once, so there were a lot of places we wanted to go and we got to most of them. By the time we said good-bye to Dave at five o'clock in front of our hotel, we were looking forward to a quiet evening. Our ship was scheduled to sail early the next morning and we meant to catch up on our sleep. Besides, my feet ached and Rusty's were almost killing her. She had made the fatal error of wearing new shoes on our long trek.

"All in the world I want to do," she moaned as we staggered across the lobby, "is take a hot bath and go to bed."

But as we stopped at the desk for our key, the clerk fixed us with a disapproving look and announced that someone had been trying to reach Miss Stanley all day long.

"Me?" Rusty was incredulous. "I don't know anyone here!"

"Someone knows you," the clerk said drily. Already Rusty's charm was beginning to soften him up. He almost smiled, adding, "He's phoned at least a dozen times, leaving no message, but saying he'll call back later. Will you be in for a while?"

"Oh, yes," Rusty said feelingly. "For quite a while!"

As soon as the elevator doors closed behind us, we took off our shoes and padded down the corridor in our stocking feet. Scarcely had we reached our room when the phone started ringing. Rusty dropped her pumps and flew to answer it.

Only a little over an hour later, we were on our way out once more. There had been time for baths, for a change of clothes, especially shoes. We were feeling much better.

Rusty's persistent caller, Jerry, had proved to be a very good friend of hers from Iowa. He was in New York with another young man and had made the trip especially in order to see Rusty off. But, once here, he had been stymied by the fact that he had no idea where she was staying. And there are so many hotels in New York! However, recalling having heard Rusty mention my name and the town I came from, he had called my parents long-distance and thus learned the name of our hotel. Talk about ingenuity! Why he hadn't simply phoned Rusty's parents, I was to learn later.

It was a very gay evening. There were four of us for Jerry had brought a friend, Pete. We rode the Staten

Island Ferry—as if we wouldn't have a long enough ship ride starting tomorrow. We walked along Broadway, infinitely more glamorous by night. We went dancing at several not too expensive places with loads of atmosphere.

We got back to our hotel around midnight—we with our big plans for getting to bed early! I felt guilty keeping the lights on till I had written a letter to Brad. But even after I'd turned them off, Rusty and I lay talking for hours. It was then I learned that Jerry was one of the main reasons her parents had let her go abroad.

"We've dated off and on for such a long time," Rusty said rather sadly in the darkness. "My parents don't feel he's the right man for me—for that matter, neither do I. But he is so attractive and they're worried for fear I might weaken sometime and decide to marry him."

"And might you?" I asked.

"Not a chance," Rusty said firmly. Then she giggled. "My parents would flip if they knew he'd come all this way to see me off."

Jerry was waiting in the lobby when we came down at practically the crack of dawn. Pete, he admitted, was still asleep at their hotel; it would have taken an earthquake to budge him. Jerry, however, proceeded to accompany us to the dock, where we made the disappointing discovery that our sailing had been postponed until four-thirty that afternoon. At least, Rusty and I were disappointed at the news. Jerry didn't seem to mind at all.

I tried my darnedest to fade out of the picture for the next few hours. But Rusty would have none of it. I got the impression she didn't want to spend the whole day alone with Jerry So we embarked somewhat half-heartedly on still another sight-seeing expedition. Those hours were a sort of anticlimax for us all, I think. Even for Jerry, who must have realized by this time that he was fighting a losing battle.

I felt rather sorry for him as we said good-bye at the dock. But practically as soon as my feet touched the gangplank, he slipped from my thoughts. Far too much lay ahead for the past to hold my attention. And Rusty seemed to feel the same way. And we set out to explore the ship.

By the time we reached the upper deck, gongs were sounding and a voice on the ship's loud-speaker was asking all visitors to go ashore. Somewhere a band started playing and it all seemed very festive and gay.

We expected to sail any minute, but, as things turned out, we were being unduly optimistic. People clustered at the rail, chattering and waving. The band kept on playing intermittently. We asked a young ship's officer when we'd be leaving.

"Ten-fifteen minutes," he beamed. His heavy German accent made him a bit hard to understand.

Half an hour later we asked a different officer the same question. He said, "Ten-fifteen minutes," with a Greek accent. At least Rusty and I thought it was Greek.

We waited and waited, as did everyone else. The wavers wearied and stopped waving. The chatterers sort of ran down. By the time we actually got under way, it was eight-thirty and the blue dusk had thickened to blackness. Against the dark, the lights of Manhattan were a strand of junk jewelry, stretched long and glittering behind us. Then the Statue of Liberty, flood-lighted and serene, appeared to move slowly past.

Good-bye—my lips formed the word soundlessly as I watched her go, holding her torch high above her pointed crown.

I was grateful for the touch of Rusty's shoulder against mine as we leaned on the rail and were borne smoothly out to sea on our way to new worlds, new adventures.

3

AIX-EN-PROVENCE, HERE WE COME

According to its colorful brochure, our ship was a floating hotel, capable of carrying seventy-five first class and twelve hundred tourist passengers. It had many spacious public rooms, including libraries, lounges and cocktail bars. In addition there were beauty and barber shops, children's playrooms and gift shops. Exclusive accommodations were afforded the first class, but the greater part of the ship was allotted to the passengers traveling tourist.

All this was true enough, but we learned a lot of other things about our ship during the ten-day crossing. One was that the bunks were short. My feet stuck out a good six inches beyond the end of mine unless I slept like a letter S. Rusty was too long for her bunk, too.

"Maybe," I suggested, "people used to be shorter forty years ago when this ship was built."

The ship wasn't nearly filled; there were only around five hundred passengers. I felt so sorry for that elegant little handful traveling first class. There were so many more of us tourists and we had so much more fun. True, there weren't enough ping-pong tables and the swimming pool was postage-stamp size and the free movies shown every day were mostly old ones that Rusty and I had already seen. But even so, time definitely didn't hang heavily on our hands.

It was the passengers we found intriguing. Most of them were around our age, European and male! What a delightful situation! I met people from all over Europe, many of them returning from student exchange programs in the United States. They wanted to practice their English and I was happy to oblige. Talking with Hungarians, French, Germans, Bohemians, Greeks, Irish, British, Canadians and one Ukrainian, I felt my horizons broadening by the minute. And Rusty admitted to the same sensation.

"It's so facinating," she said, "hearing all these different viewpoints, talking with people who've had such unusual backgrounds and experiences."

I agreed. "Makes me feel I've lived a very insulated sort of life. Oh, I knew a lot of foreign students at Park. But this isn't the same. Now we're in the minority, rather than they."

"Aren't you glad," Rusty said feelingly, "that we didn't come over on an American ship? There we'd have met people just like ourselves. This is so much more enlightening."

I was a bit surprised by her reaction, even though I felt that way myself. Maybe Rusty had a more inquiring mind than I had realized. Her sincerity was obvious.

Of course, we weren't the only Americans on board, but there weren't too many. We ran into just one other student who was heading for the Institute. He was Earl Bristol, a pleasant young veteran, engaged to a girl who would be studying in Madrid. He and Rusty and I didn't see a lot of each other on shipboard, but we did make plans to travel together from Le Havre, where our ship docked, to Aix-en-Provence on the southern edge of France.

As Earl put it drily, "We'll have a sort of mutual aid deal. I can help with your luggage and you two can speak French."

"No one could understand me," Rusty disclaimed. "Judy will have to get us all through."

Her words made a curious prickling feeling run down my spine. Would my two years' study of French prove adequate?

Each morning in one of the lounges a French couple conducted an informal class for those who wished to study advanced conversation. I found this quite helpful for my accent. It was also in this class that I first met Dave Schultz, a dark, rather intense young math major at Yale, now on his way to Nancy, France, for a year's study. Dave and I, early in our association, discovered a mutual passion—bridge.

Dave was my opponent in our first game. After that we teamed up as partners. He played a consistently sound, razor-sharp game, which inspired me to outdo myself. He was also interested in sociology and this gave us ground for some fascinating discussions. We would sit by the hour on the sunny deck, alone or with a group of others, talking and talking. The clarity and originality of his ideas fascinated me. There was nothing at all romantic about our relationship. Dave was quite serious about a girl back home and he knew about Brad. But this didn't stop us from becoming good friends.

I wrote Brad about Dave in the long, day-to-day letter which I would mail when we docked. Brad wouldn't mind our friendship I knew. We had planned to date other people during our separation. It would have been foolish not to. I wished Brad could have known Dave, too. He'd have liked him as well as I did.

When Dave suggested we write while we were in France, naturally I agreed. "It would be fun to compare impressions."

"Maybe we could get together sometime," he went on.

"Nancy's a long way from Aix," I reminded.

"But we're both planning to travel during vacations," he said. "Maybe we can work something out."

"It would be fun," I admitted. "I hope we can."

Rusty's devastating charm kept her constantly surrounded by enthusiastic admirers. She danced in one or another of the ship's lounges every night. That some of these ardent companions might be getting a little hard to handle, I had no idea until the evening near the end of our voyage when Rusty confided in me, "I don't dare go out on deck alone after dark with Franz. He's so—intense!"

"Your paths will part in a few more days," I reminded.

"That's what I'm figuring on," Rusty said. "In the meantime, no deserted decks in the moonlight!"

Early on the morning of September twelfth, we sighted land. You can't imagine what a thing like that means, unless you've spent days and days on a churning, billowing, rolling gray ocean. Even when the sun shines and the ocean is calm and blue, it looks very big and empty. So the distant shore of Ireland was a welcome sight.

We didn't get very close to Ireland, but we did dock

at Southampton around noon. Everyone clustered excitedly at the rails as we came into port. Some passengers were disembarking; there were farewells to be said to people who seemed like old friends after ten days' acquaintance. Those of us who were going on to Le Havre weren't permitted to set foot on English soil. But there was a great bag of mail going ashore to be started on the long way home to family and friends. Soon the busy little tugs were shoving us around again and we headed out into the channel once more.

"It won't be long now," I said to Rusty, as we leaned on the rail in the pallid sunshine, watching the coast of England slip away. "A few more hours and we'll be in France."

"Nine o'clock, I heard," Rusty answered. "Does it give you a strange feeling to think of actually getting there?"

"Very strange," I admitted. "This old tub almost seems like home, we've been on her so long."

The wind caught Rusty's bright hair and blew it across her face. She brushed it aside, murmuring, "All the kids we've met and had such fun with—we'll probably never see them again."

"I guess that's the way it is on ocean voyages."

"France," Rusty's voice was soft. "It's always sounded so glamorous to me. But when I realize we'll actually be there tonight, right in the thick of all those millions of people who don't even speak English—well, I get cold feet a little."

"So do I." What was the sense in denying it? "But we'll manage all right. There'll be a boat-train to take us to Paris—and Dave will be with us that far. He speaks

French very well. From Paris all we have to do is get the right train for Marseilles and then get from there to Aix—" my voice sort of ran down. It didn't sound exactly simple.

"I'm glad you know French so well," Rusty said admiringly.

I appreciated the compliment. If only, I hoped, the French people agreed with her opinion of my linguistic powers!

Our ship was three hours late in reaching Le Havre. It was midnight by the time we experienced the odd sensation of solid ground under our feet. The pier was a great echoing place, almost empty except for us disembarking passengers and a few sleepy-looking customs officials and porters. I caught disjointed words and phrases in the babble of French all about. If they would only talk more slowly, I thought, I could understand them so much better. I was grateful for Dave's presence as he and Rusty and Earl and I proceeded to locate our suitcases and present the necessary forms to the proper officials. They didn't even bother to open our luggage, simply stamped the forms and waved us on.

"But what about our trunks?" I asked. They were nowhere in sight and both Rusty and I were beginning to grow anxious.

I had asked the question in French, somewhat hesitantly. But the official understood me. However, he addressed his answer to Dave, apparently feeling that this was man's business.

"We'll have to wait till they show up and check them through," Dave told us. I was thrilled that his translation of the customs official's answer matched my own.

"But how long?" Rusty yawned.

The yawn was contagious. We were all pretty tired.

"Who knows?" Earl said glumly.

We stood around, griping, growing more and more fidgety. Gradually quite a large clump of Americans gathered about us, all equally trunkless and concerned. A minor ship's officer approached to explain that the boat-train hadn't been able to wait for our late arrival, but that we would be taken to Paris by bus instead. "There's plenty of time, though," he assured us. "Don't worry about being left."

"But what about our trunks?" several voices demanded.

"They'll be along," he said vaguely and drifted away.

Several French porters hovered nearby, very picturesque in their jaunty caps and little green aprons. At first they were cheerful, laughing and making jokes about our predicament, but at length they, too, became annoyed with the delay. Some of them informed us confidentially that we didn't have to wait for our trunks, that these could be checked through customs without our being there, and sent on to our destination. But this wasn't what the officials had said. It was all very confusing and we were growing wearier by the minute.

The more we discussed it the stronger grew our belief that the porters were probably right. Trunks might well be sent through customs all the time without the owners being there, but, since this wasn't legal, the officials couldn't come right out and admit it. I'd heard the French were like that.

"I wish they'd make up their minds," Rusty said in a small voice.

She had had polio as a child, I knew. And while she had made a complete recovery, her leg muscles were a little weak, so that when she grew overly tired they bothered her. Seeing how pale she looked now, I felt a protective urge rise in me. "Isn't there anything we can do?" I demanded of no one in particular.

Luckily the ship's officer who had spoken to us earlier came up just then. Everyone fell on him with accusations and queries, but he dismissed all these with an airy wave of the hand.

"Do not trouble yourselves," he soothed. "It is all arranged. Your trunks will be passed through customs later and sent on to you as quickly as possible. Okay?" He couldn't have been around a bunch of Americans for ten days without picking up that last word, I realized, yet it sounded odd on his lips.

"But if that's the case," Earl demanded, "what have we been hanging around here for all this time?"

"The bus," the officer explained with a placating smile. "It is just now ready to depart for Paris. Come, everyone."

Just before we staggered out of the customs' house and into the moonlit shadows of our first night—or rather morning!—in France, I looked at my watch. I was so sleepy, I had a hard time focusing my eyes on its little dial, but I finally managed to see that its hands were pointing to exactly two-thirty.

4

WE ARRIVE

I never remembered much about that bus trip from Le Havre to Paris, since I slept through most of it. The bus was comfortable enough, but the roads were very bumpy. We went jolting and bouncing through the night; part of the time my head was on Dave's shoulder, part of the time his was on mine. We were both too tired to care who supported whom. Eventually dawn broke beyond the windows just as we reached the outskirts of Paris. And I found my sleepiness dissipated by this first glimpse of the city the very name of which is synonymous with romance.

It didn't seem particularly romantic at six o'clock in the morning, Dave and I agreed. But there was no denying that the narrow streets twisting off from either side of the broad road the bus traveled looked picturesque. The buildings seemed different than big city buildings in the United States. They were narrower, not nearly so tall, much older except for an occasional new and modern one, which looked a little out of place. The few people on the streets at this early hour were dressed the same way people dressed back home. But the signs on the shops seemed odd to me, even though I could translate them perfectly well and knew that "Coiffeur" meant barber, or hairdresser, and "Patisserie" meant bakery and "Librairie" meant bookshop.

I was still craning my neck, trying not to miss anything, when the bus jerked to a stop at the terminal. We all piled out, bag and baggage, looking half-asleep and rather badly rumpled. This was the final parting of the ways for most of us. Everyone rushed about, saying, "Good-bye" and "Good luck," and trying to find out how to head for his own particular destination.

Dave said, "Let's make it au revoir instead of so long, shall we? It seems more fitting here." He pressed my hand hard, adding, "I'll write—and be sure you answer."

"I will," I promised, hating to see him go.

He had to catch his train for Nancy, about two hundred miles east of Paris. Rusty, Earl and I had a much longer train trip ahead of us, in an entirely different direction. As Dave strode away, I felt a queer sinking sensation in my tummy. Now we were on our own and my French was going to get a real workout.

We found that our train would leave from the Gare de Lyon and that we'd need a cab to reach there. I was surprised, but pleased, that the driver understood me when I told him where we wanted to go. On our way, he remarked casually that it was a beautiful morning and I answered, "Yes, isn't it?" before I did a slight double-take and realized he was speaking English—heavily accented, not too easy to understand, but English nonetheless.

"Hey, he speaks English!" Earl exclaimed in surprise.

"Little bit," the driver admitted, beaming at us across

his shoulder as he passed a lumbering truck. "You Americans, I bet." At our nods, he continued, "Students? I think so. Lots Americans," he told us, darting past a scattering bevy of pedestrians, "come to school here. Is good. Where you go to study?"

When we told him he said soulfully, "Ah, Aix-en-Provence she is beautiful. But no so beautiful as Paree. Why you don't stay here? Is so much bigger."

By the time we had convinced him it was too late to change all our plans, he pulled up in front of the station with a flourish. To Earl's query of, "How much?" he responded, "Seven hundred francs."

It sounded like a lot of money till we broke it down mentally and realized it amounted to less than two dollars. We paid him off with some of the big, bright-colored bills we had acquired, at Mr. Maza's suggestion, before leaving the United States and made our way into the Gare de Lyon. The sinking sensation I had experienced before hit me harder than ever. Railway stations are always such big, bustling, impersonal places. And here I was, entirely responsible for getting the three of us through this one and onto the right train.

Rusty chose this moment to say in a rather plaintive tone, "I'm starving. I hope we can eat before train time."

"So do I," Earl seconded.

How could they think of food at a time like this, I wondered? Then I realized that maybe the queer feeling in my tummy might be partly due to hunger. After all, none of us had eaten since dinnertime last night. And it was now well after seven.

"Let's find out about our train first," I said. "Maybe we'll have to eat on it."

"Do they have diners on French trains?" Earl asked.

"We'll have to find out about that, too." Purposefully I walked up to what seemed to be an Information Desk and started asking questions. And, wonder of wonders, the man understood me. Oh, he knew I wasn't French, all right. But at least he grasped what I was trying somewhat haltingly to find out.

"Our train leaves at nine-fifteen," I reported back to Rusty and Earl. "And it's due in Marseilles at six-thirty tonight. From there we get a bus to Aix-en-Provence, about an hour's ride."

"So long?" Rusty sighed.

"How about breakfast?" Earl asked.

"We can get that here in the station, right over that way."

The station restaurant seemed clean, if plain. Rusty and I studied the menu, translating the various foods into English for Earl's benefit. We saw nothing like bacon or eggs or milk or cereal.

"Guess it'll have to be coffee and rolls," Earl said. "That's about all there is."

Rusty nodded. "Sounds good to me."

I didn't like coffee. Yet I couldn't relish the thought of rolls and nothing else. Down near the bottom of the menu I discovered a familiar, thoroughly American word that reached out to me like the hand of an old friend.

When the waitress approached for our orders, I told her, "Trois croissants,"—that was three rolls. "Deux cafés,"—that was two coffees. "And one—I mean un Coca-Cola."

Rusty and Earl burst into laughter. "Coke for breakfast," Rusty said, when she could speak. "That's the funniest thing I ever heard of."

I was laughing, too. "If they don't have cows here it's not my fault. I have to find something to take the place of milk."

The warm crusty croissants we were served a few minutes later were delicious. Not sweet like American breakfast rolls, they had a delicate flavor all their own. We ordered seconds before we were half-finished with the first ones. By the time we left the little restaurant, we felt much better.

Our train left promptly on schedule. It was very modern and fast and beautifully appointed, but quite different from the trains we were accustomed to. It was divided into compartments, each seating eight people. Our compartment was shared by a family, so typically French that it seemed unbelievable. There were a mother and father and two children, around two and five. When the parents heard us speaking English, they were intrigued and asked at once if we could speak French.

I admitted that I could, a little, and they were delighted to learn I had taken the trouble to study their language before coming to their country. They were very patient with my mistakes and tried to talk slowly for my benefit. But then they would get interested in the subject we were discussing and start racing along again at a mad clip. They asked a few questions about the United States, which I answered as fully as I could. Then they began to tell me about France and their manner became much more enthusiastic. I got the impression that the French feel a little sorry for anyone who wasn't born there. They don't blame you for it, but their attitude indicates clearly they're happy such a dreadful thing didn't happen to them.

At lunchtime the French woman had her husband take down their suitcase and she proceeded to get out a bottle of wine, a long crusty-looking loaf of bread and a bag with cheese and fruit in it. While the three of us tried not to stare, fascinated, the family ate, breaking off hunks of bread, which they ate with the cheese, and washing it down with drinks from the wine bottle. All of them seemed to enjoy their meal, even the two-year-old. Once the bread dropped on the floor, but this didn't perturb them. The woman simply wiped it off on her skirt and they went on eating and drinking with undiminished appetite.

There was a diner, very elegant and terribly expensive-looking. But before we were driven to patronizing it, the train stopped in some city or other. And we had time to get out and buy sandwiches and candy bars from a platform vendor.

All of us slept away a part of the long afternoon. Our French family left us somewhere along the way with a friendly adieu. Part of the time we watched the spectacular scenery flashing past the windows, mountains and rivers and dense forests already lightly touched with the colors of autumn. Sometimes the train ran through pleasant farmland, not so very different from that back in Illinois and Iowa, Rusty and I agreed.

"Except," I said, "back home they'd be harvesting with big machines, instead of by hand, with only a horse to help."

The cities where the train stopped weren't so unusual, but the little villages it rushed through without pausing looked fascinating. Once we glimpsed women washing clothes in a narrow, fast-flowing stream. And little boys in smocks occasionally stood in country lanes to see the train pass.

"Back home they'd be wearing blue jeans," Rusty remarked. "But the dreaming, entranced look on their faces is the same everywhere, I guess."

We reached Marseilles at six-thirty, tired, rumpled, not too clean and practically starving. Again the responsibility of getting us safely onto the right transportation scared me a little. It was a relief to find out that we could get a trolley-bus for Aix almost immediately, even if this did mean we'd have to postpone dinner. We were all agreed that we'd enjoy eating a lot more once we'd actually reached our destination.

We dozed through most of that last lap of our long journey. From the station, we called Mr. Maza, after something of a struggle with the French operator. The sound of his hearty American voice was music in my ears. "Stay right there," he commanded. "I'll be over to get you in ten minutes."

And he was!

Tanned and not very old-looking despite his white hair, he was quite distinguished in looks and manner as he came hurrying toward us. My first impression was of a gentle friendliness that seemed to reach out and wrap us about, making us feel welcome and safe. When he found we hadn't eaten, he took us in his little car to La Taverne, a restaurant very popular with students both for its food and prices. The sight of the word *bifteck* on the menu nearly convulsed us. We were definitely a little slap-happy by that time. It proved to be quite the toughest steak we had ever eaten, although the vegetables that accompanied it were delicious. We finished our meal off with French pastries, also delectable, while Mr. Maza sat with us, talking and drinking Espresso coffee. This was served in a tiny cup and looked thick and black enough to float a spoon.

"Can't you get milk to drink at all?" I asked forlornly.

"I shouldn't advise it," Mr. Maza cautioned. "The milk here isn't pasteurized properly and one takes a chance drinking it."

"How about water?" I asked.

"In good restaurants, yes," he answered. "Not otherwise. But there are various bottled waters available which are safe. And the wines of the region are excellent and quite mild."

I could see plainly my eating habits were going to require adjusting. But I was too tired to cope with the problem tonight.

When we were finished, Mr. Maza took Rusty and me to the Pavillon du Cloitre, where we were to live. He introduced us to Madame Lupin, a plump, motherly-looking sort of person, who ran the place. We thanked Mr. Maza and said goodnight to him and Earl, then followed Madame Lupin up an iron-railed flight of stairs to our room. We were practically staggering by that time, having been awake some thirty-eight hours, except for fitful snatches of sleep on trains and buses. Madame bustled about, talking in animated French, fluffing up pillows and straightening the mirror and pointing out our suitcases, which Mr. Maza had arranged to have brought from the bus station.

But Rusty and I were in no condition to appreciate

the beauties or deplore the deficiencies of this room that was to be our home for the next ten months. All we really saw was the two beds. And into these, having got rid of Madame at last and washed ourselves sketchily at the lavatory in the corner, we proceeded to crawl gratefully.

5

ORIENTATION WEEK

Our dorm, we found, was not a part of the Institute or the University at all. European colleges seldom supply living accommodations, they simply approve certain boarding houses. Luckily for us the Pavillon was very nice. It was on a narrow side street in the old section of town and one entered it through an ancient gray stone arch and across a fairly spacious courtyard. This courtyard was a mess when we arrived, filled with piles of sand and bricks and lumber left over from the building of the Pavillon itself. In fact, building operations were by no means finished when we moved in. The first two floors were completed, except for some decorating, but up on the third floor we could hear workmen hammering and sawing away for several weeks.

Just inside the front door was a large room, furnished with modern straight-backed chairs and tables, a sort of cross between a lounge and breakfast room. Breakfast, Rusty and I knew, was included with our room for the price of eleven hundred francs a month. According to the rate of exchange then in effect, this amounted roughly to twenty-three dollars. Breakfast, we were to discover, meant something quite different in France than it did back home. It consisted of tea or coffee, delicious crusty bread and some sort of preserves or jelly. No fruit juice, no cereal or milk, no bacon and eggs. Luckily, neither of us had ever gone in for a very heavy breakfast.

At first, we toyed with the idea of living with a French family, instead of staying on at the Pavillon. Mr. Maza said this could be arranged. But after talking with some students who had tried it, we decided to stay put. Families who took in roomers, we learned, often consisted entirely of older people. And they set strict limits as to how often one could wash, iron, or take baths. Madame assured us that, once the French students arrived in November, we could be reshuffled so that each American girl might have a French roommate. This appealed to both Rusty and me.

In the meantime, we settled quite happily into our room on the second floor. It was fairly large, with a tiled floor and walls painted a soft green. There were two beds and a double dresser, a small, but adequate closet, two chairs and a sort of shelf-desk that extended all the way across the window wall. In addition to our own lavatory, there were toilets and shower-rooms just down the hall. And Madame placed no restriction on the number of showers we could take, or how often we might use the laundry room downstairs. However, some other students warned us she wouldn't be so lenient when the Pavillon became filled up later on.

"But why?" I asked.

"Because," a girl named Joan told me, "this is France and electricity is expensive. And it takes electricity to heat water and operate irons. And no Frenchwoman, including Madame, runs a boarding house for fun. You'll find out."

Time was to prove her right. But just at first Rusty and I suspected she was maligning our landlady.

That first morning we read our mail—I had three lovely fat letters from Brad, as well as several from my family— then showered luxuriously and washed our hair. Next we pressed our clothes, wrinkled by too long confinement in suitcases, and put them away in closet and dresser. Our trunks, to be sent by railway express from Le Havre, hadn't arrived yet, but, according to Mr. Maza, should be along soon. We had a couple of days' grace before Orientation Week began, so we decided to use this time in exploring our new surroundings.

Rusty and I fell in love with Aix-en-Provence at first sight. A travel agent would no doubt describe the town as quaint and charming, because it is. Yet it isn't a manufactured charm, built up to impress tourists. And its quaintness is utterly genuine, a result of the inhabitants' liking for old ways and the less casual customs of a more leisurely time. Far back in antiquity, it was a Roman health resort and there are still ruins of the old baths on the hills around the town. The elegant golden limestone houses that line its narrow, twisting streets were built mostly in the seventeenth and eighteenth centuries. There are quantities of tiny shops, each selling its own particular product.

"No super-markets," Rusty observed. "To buy food for a meal, you'd have to go half a dozen places, one for meat and another for bread and another for butter and another for vegetables."

I nodded. "Think of the time it would take. And yet nobody seems to be hurrying."

We passed an outdoor market and paused to admire the bright fresh colors of the fruits and vegetables displayed on long tables. Women wandered about, selecting things and tucking them into their baskets or string shopping bags. Strolling on, we turned a corner and stopped of one accord, thrilled by the sight ahead.

This was the Cours Mirabeau, the broadest, the loveliest boulevard in all of Aix, even in all of France some people say. Giant sycamore trees met overhead, their gray-and-dull-green-mottled trunks rising on either side of the wide pavement. Cafés, their small round tables and bright-colored umbrellas dotting the sidewalks, seemed to be doing a flourishing business. Occasionally great golden leaves drifted softly down to rest on the heads or shoulders of the patrons. Nearby a large old fountain splashed and tinkled, not the first fountain we had seen by any means. But this one was more impressive than the smaller ones in other squares. Later, we were to learn that the Cours Mirabeau really came to life in the late afternoon, when it was the favorite promenade of the townspeople and students, too. Here one walked slowly speaking to one's friends, stopping for a pastry at one of the numerous sidewalk cafés, or just savoring the serene beauty of the deepening dusk.

That first afternoon, Rusty and I walked up one side of the Cours and down the other. It is only a few blocks long, yet it took us quite a while, so fascinating were the little shops, with their window displays of everything imaginable. We succumbed to the lure of one shop, where enormous quantities of hard candy and caramels were displayed simply but effectively in bushel baskets.

From the Cours we walked toward the University, several blocks away and in a newer part of town. Here the houses, with lovely gardens and large courtyards, seemed richer than in the area around the Institute. The University buildings were mostly modern and quite large. Law, art and liberal arts were taught here, while students specializing in medicine or science attended the other branch of the University located in Marseilles. With classes not yet in session the buildings had a lonely, deserted air about them.

"Just think," I mused, "not this semester, but next, we'll be having some of our classes there."

"*If* my French is equal to it," Rusty amended drily. "You don't have to worry, though."

Ever since I had got us safely from Le Havre to Aix, she seemed convinced that I spoke French like a native.

On our way back to the Pavillon, we got lost several times. This was easy to do, since the streets soon grew narrow and twisting and often seemed to change names at an intersection for no discernible reason. The sidewalks became narrow, too, so that one often had to step off into the street to pass others going in the opposite direction. This could be dangerous, we immediately discovered. The French people might walk in a slow and leisurely manner, but when mounted they acted quite differently. Motor bikes and scooters, regular bikes ridden by young and old, and small, but speedy foreign cars went whizzing past at a dizzy clip. And pedestrians were expected to get out of the way fast!

Within a few days, though, Rusty and I knew our

way around pretty well, at least in the area near the Pavillon. And the big stone building, with its graceful iron grillwork and the French flag flying in front, which housed the Institute, became a familiar landmark for us. It was only a few blocks from our dorm, but our way there led past a fascinating outdoor market, where fresh fruit tempted us, under an arch where we often saw lovers kissing each other good-bye, and across several narrow alleys where lean cats prowled, or lay sleeping in the sunshine. All very interesting.

Our first week at the Institute was an Orientation period, with Mr. Maza telling us how to live in Aix and answering our questions. He also delivered a few clarifying lectures on French politics. A French placement test climaxed Orientation Week, but didn't prove too difficult. Actually, it was all a little dull, but we were grateful for the opportunity it gave us to get acquainted with our fellow students. To our surprise, we found that there were only about twenty-five of us all together. This was the Institute's first year and it would undoubtedly grow. But somehow, all of us had expected there would be more students.

Most of the people we met at school seemed pleasant enough, still I was a bit disappointed in the men. There were more males than females, that part was all right. But there just didn't seem to be anyone terribly exciting. The most promising of the lot was Steve McConnell. He was a tall, fairly blond young man with wonderfully broad shoulders and a nice smile. His family now lived in Germany, where his father was with the American army. Steve was originally from Colorado and just a trace of a western drawl made his way of speaking seem slow and endearingly gentle. He was quite attractive, Rusty and I agreed. The only trouble, so far as I was concerned, was that he seemed much more taken with Rusty than with me.

Not that I minded, really. Brad loomed too large in my thoughts to be easily displaced. I missed him so, now that the excitement of the trip was over and life was beginning to seem more normal, that at times I ached with loneliness. Each time I saw his familiar, almost undecipherable scrawl on a letter, my heart did a little shaken flip-flop. And I'd dash up to my room to read it, like a thirst-crazed wanderer in the desert rushing for a water hole. Brad missed me as much as I missed him, I gathered from his letters.

Mr. Maza did all he could to make our first days in a foreign country agreeable and to ward off homesickness. He and his wife gave a tea for the students in their pleasant apartment. He told us of a local pool, where we enjoyed swimming while the warm autumn weather continued. He suggested possible eating places. The difficulty was that the University cafeteria, where arrangements had been made for us to eat regularly, would not open until the University did.

In the meantime, we tried several restaurants, including La Taverne, where we had eaten tough *bifteck* the night of our arrival. The food was tasty enough almost everywhere, but there were more starches than Rusty and I liked and we found the meat rather greasy. Dinner was the midday meal in France; even stores and offices closed for two hours at noon, so that employees could go home to eat. Rusty and I, as well as some of the other Americans, fell into the habit of buying fresh fruit at the outdoor market, supplementing it with bread and cheese, then finishing off our picnic with pastries and tea or coffee at a sidewalk café. But we didn't feel we were indulging in a very well-balanced diet. And we were glad when Mr. Maza suggested, and then made the necessary arrangements, for the girls to eat at a local convent.

The nuns, serene-faced in their black habits and wide snowy wimples, made us very welcome. Children attending the convent school found us a source of never-ending curiosity. But they were polite enough about it, except in one respect. Mr. Maza had informed us that Oxfords were the correct footwear for college girls in France, and so everyone had brought a pair from the United States. But the convent school children stared in pop-eyed amazement at our feet and then went off into gales of giggles. We were to learn that Mr. Maza had been mistaken in this respect, that Oxfords in France are considered proper only on young children and very old ladies. So ours faded out of the picture quite soon.

The convent food proved perfectly delicious. Simple, yet so tastefully prepared, that we all gorged ourselves the first day or so, after our rather eccentric preceding diet. Almost every girl became ill to some degree, although I was lucky enough to be upset only slightly by my shameless overeating. The nuns were so distressed to hear of our problem that some of us tried, in our hesitant French, to explain to them that it wasn't their food that was at fault, but our appetites. After we thought we had made the situation clear, one of them turned to another and said in French, so rapidly that I suppose she thought we couldn't understand, "These poor Americans! They couldn't afford to eat in the restaurants and so they were starving to death before they came here." All of the sweet-faced nuns regarded us so pityingly, we let it go at that.

With the arrival of our trunks, Rusty and I began to feel quite settled. But one night as we were getting ready for bed, she remarked, "I never knew the first week of school to pass so quietly. Back at Iowa, we'd just be winding up rush."

"Was it fun?" I asked. "Hash sessions and all that?"

"Oh, sure," Rusty nodded, "in a hectic sort of way." Her tone sounded nostalgic. "There weren't any sororities or fraternities at your college, were there?"

"No," I told her, "but there were lots of social clubs and things to do all the time, dances, parties—" I began to feel nostalgic, too. So far our entertainment had consisted of two French movies, a couple of swims at the pool, the Mazas' tea, several walks and quite a lot of reading and letter writing. And no dates at all.

Rusty sighed. "I have a hunch that's what I'm going to miss most over here—social activities."

Mr. Maza had explained that European colleges were set up to educate their students, not to entertain them. Actually, I felt, we'd be better off next week when classes started and we were busier. But I wasn't sure Rusty would find this thought consoling.

"Maybe," I suggested not too optimistically, "things will pick up when the French students get here."

"Maybe," Rusty agreed.

If they didn't, I couldn't help feeling, it was going to be rather a long year. . . .

6

A LONG WALK

The first few days of classes, we had so much homework it seemed we'd never be able to keep up with it. I don't know whether our professors were trying to impress us with the idea that they meant business and would permit no goofing off, or whether the deluge just seemed so overwhelming because the only studying I'd done all summer was some boning up on my French.

"What are they trying to do, swamp us?" Rusty complained.

"Maybe they heard we had too much time on our hands."

All of our classes were in English, except one in French lit and grammar. But our professors were French, men who had lectured and taught in the United States and England. At first things were in quite a state of upheaval. Books we were to study hadn't arrived yet. Some of the professors were away, giving Baccalaureate exams to French students in other parts of the country, so that schedules had to be temporarily rearranged. It was aggravating to be given vague assignments when there was only one book available for a whole class. But soon the kinks straightened out and a regular routine was established. And rather to Rusty's and my surprise, we weren't nearly as rushed as we had expected to be. As the initial confusion lessened, neither of us found our studies any great problem and we were able to keep up with our assignments quite easily.

"Somehow, I wish we'd stayed busier," I confided.

And Rusty agreed, "So do I, although I never thought I'd live to see the day I'd be *craving* more homework."

The thing we were both missing was a real honest-to-goodness date. We admitted it frankly. Never had either of us gone so long without a little masculine attention. The men at the Institute were friendly enough, but none of them had asked either of us out. Some of them were engaged, some too broke to do much dating and some just weren't interested. Whenever we ran into Steve McConnell, he was quite attentive to Rusty, but so far he hadn't done anything constructive about the situation. It was a thoroughly deplorable state of affairs.

By Friday night we were feeling bored and frustrated. After our homework was done, we sat around bemoaning the lack of social life. You can spend just so much time talking and writing letters, then you begin to feel sorry for yourself. The bad angle was that there seemed no prospect of anything to do in Aix except go to movies, or go to an occasional play or concert. There would be few school dances or parties, such as we were used to, no Student Union to spend one's spare time in, hobnobbing with friends. It would be different during vacations. Then we could travel. We had already begun to discuss going to Switzerland over Thanksgiving weekend, to Italy for Christmas, Spain between semesters and probably Paris at Easter time. But it was the immediate present that had us down.

"In France," Mr. Maza had told us, "students make their own fun. Pleasures are more simple, not so organized as in America."

We had nothing whatever against simple pleasures. It was just that we didn't know where to make a start.

Saturday afternoon Rusty was involved in an art field trip, so I went for a long walk alone. I decided to leave the town behind and head out into the countryside. It was quite hilly and the soil was almost shrimp-colored, a sort of clay that probably wasn't very fertile. Irrigation ditches divided the fields. I saw a horse in a fenced pasture and my heart lifted. I love horses and had one of my own for several years. I felt a mad urge to climb the fence and ride this one, but I confined myself to going over and patting his outstretched nose. He responded by licking my palm, just as my horse used to do. The familiar touch of his tongue made me feel all choky and I walked on quickly, not wanting to dissolve into tears right out on a public road.

A bit farther on I encountered a red-faced peasant woman having trouble with her motor bike. The chain had come loose, so I held the bike upright for her while she reattached it and she thanked me warmly. By saying very little, I think I left her with the impression that I was French, too. This gave me quite a thrill. A little farther on I came upon an extraordinary sight. Several miles ahead, across a vista of trees and valleys, loomed an enormous gray and white mountain. I stood quite still for a time, struck by the rugged grandeur of the great peak against the bright blue sky. Something vaguely familiar about it nagged at me. Then I realized I must be very near the spot where Cézanne painted his "Mont Ste. Victoire," which hangs in the Metropolitan Museum of Art.

It was hard to turn away from such beauty, but I finally managed to. On my way home a weather-beaten old man working in a vegetable field said, "Bon jour, Mademoiselle," and assured me that his tiny barking dog wouldn't bite. His friendliness was very pleasant and heartening. A while later two boys around ten or so came along, riding one bicycle. They said, "Allo," and, when I responded, they stopped and asked me politely if I was English, from London. I couldn't resist letting them think so. It was so nice to be considered English, whom the French like, rather than American, whom they usually don't for some reason.

Back in Aix, I strolled unhurriedly toward the Pavillon. Somehow my walk had done me good. I felt relaxed and happy. The sights I had seen, the people I had talked with, all contributed in some way to a release from the tension that had gripped me when I set out. After all, I realized, something didn't have to be happening every minute to make life enjoyable. There could be satisfaction in small things, simple pleasures. Of course, one lived differently in Europe. I had expected that; it was one of the reasons I had wanted to come here. So why should I get all tied up in knots over a little thing like a dearth of dates, a slowed-down social pace? One just had to learn to adapt oneself, to live in the present with quiet appreciation. And I felt I'd taken a big step forward in that respect this afternoon.

Rusty had enjoyed her field trip. She told me all about it while we got ready to go to the convent for dinner. "And you know what?" she finished. "Some of us have a big excursion all planned for tomorrow. I told them you'd like to go, too."

"What sort of an excursion?" I asked.

"To Avignon and Nimes," Rusty answered. "We can go by bus and there'll be half a dozen or more of us, girls and men. They're terribly historical places and they have bull fights at Nimes—"

"I'll skip the bull fight," I interrupted firmly, "but I'd love all the rest of it." After all, I felt, simple pleasures could be appreciated, but that didn't mean you had to pass up anything more exciting that came along. . . .

Eight of us caught an early morning bus for Avignon the next day. We were all in a gay mood, speeding along through the lovely countryside, pausing in picturesque villages to take on and discharge passengers. Everyone regarded us with lively interest when they heard us speaking a foreign language.

"That's the thing I can't get used to over here," one of the boys admitted, chuckling. "We're the foreigners!"

It was rather an odd sensation.

In Avignon, we had enough time between buses to do a good deal of sight-seeing. We explored the narrow streets of the ancient walled city and visited the palace where the popes lived during their exile from Rome in the fourteenth century. This was a massive white stone building, with in-cut crosses, through which, according to the brochure we were given, arrows could be shot in times of danger. We climbed a high hill to view the remaining arches of the bridge built across the Rhone by St. Bénézet in the twelfth century, the famous Pont d'Avignon of the old song. It only extends halfway across the river, quite a bizarre effect. Back in the main square of the town once more, we were mobbed by a crowd of beggar children. One of the Institute men had made the mistake of using his camera, thus branding himself a tourist. But we escaped by giving the little waifs a few francs and caught our bus for Nimes.

We reached our destination a little before noon and went at once to the Arena. This was a sort of stadium, built on the ruins of the Roman original and exactly like it. Here the others checked up on tickets to the bull fight and found they would have to return at one o'clock, two hours before the fight was due to start, in order to get decent seats. They tried to persuade me to go, too, but the very idea made me feel a little sick. We all found a pleasant shady park and there we ate our lunch, which, in true French fashion, we'd brought with us. The bread and cheese and fruit tasted delicious and the mild wine we drank with it seemed scarcely more potent than a soft drink. Afterwards, the rest of the crowd went to the bull fight and I saw Nimes.

It was a fascinating old city through which I walked, exploring two cathedrals with vaulted ceilings and lovely stained glass windows. In the large park I admired the fountains and formal gardens and the impressive statues set in niches of green. Down a winding path I came upon an ancient Roman bath. It was easy to imagine Romans of Caesar's time descending the moss-covered stairs into the green water. At one end of the park was a large hill, thick with pines, at the top of which was a Roman tower. From up there I could see the whole city spread out below. I even looked wistfully off toward the west and wondered what Brad was doing just then and whether he might be thinking of me.

At five o'clock I met the others. Some of them had liked the bull fight, some hadn't, and most of the girls still looked a bit green. Since there was no bus back to Aix until midnight, we decided to take a ten o'clock train to Marseilles. We had a leisurely dinner and then walked around, stopping at sidewalk cafés for pastries and coffee. Our trip back seemed rather long, although we enlivened it with much talk and laughter. Rusty and I were half asleep as we stumbled up the stairs to our room. But the day had been great fun, we agreed.

"It was a nice crowd, wasn't it?" Rusty whispered.

I nodded. "You and Steve seemed to hit it off just fine."

Rusty smiled. "I like him. He improves on acquaintance."

I was glad for her. I only wished one of the men we'd been with had impressed me that way. Why had I ever begun to think about Brad on that pine-covered hilltop in Nimes, I asked myself? Now I couldn't get him out of my mind. And pleasant as the day had been, none of my companions seemed remotely capable of making me forget Brad, even temporarily.

I sighed. *C'est la vie*, I told myself philosophically. Then I stopped so suddenly there in the hallway outside our bedroom door that Rusty bumped into me. I hadn't thought, That's life, as I would have a few weeks earlier. The amazing realization struck me full force. I had begun to think in French!

7

SURPRISE VISITOR

Gradually the man situation began to improve. Not that I was dating regularly, or had found anyone really special. But Rusty and I and a small blond girl from Missouri named Joan Thomas got into the pleasant habit of doing something almost every week-end with Steve McConnell and a couple of his friends, Joe Rhodes and Nick Tilden. It might be nothing more than a walk and a stop at our favorite sidewalk café, Les Deux Garçons, which, translated, meant the Two Boys. The artist, Picasso, lived near Aix and was said to frequent this café, but we never had the luck to see him. Sometimes we took in a movie. If this happened to be an American production, with French dialogue dubbed in, we often got hysterical over the flowery French words issuing from the lips of, for instance, Marlon Brando or Gary Cooper. One Saturday night we discovered a local bistro called the Cave, a strange place reached by descending a steep flight of steps that terminated in a small, dimly lit room resembling an African hut, complete with bamboo walls and fearsome native masks. There were barrels with padded tops to sit on and a record player which, to our delight, was stocked with American music. No liquor was served and no girls were permitted to go there without men, or vice versa.

We had a ball, dancing to rock'n'roll music. Joe and I gravitated naturally together and, although he wasn't very tall, he was a good dancer. As long as we jitterbugged, I scarcely thought about Brad at all. It was only when we danced to slower, sentimental-type songs, that I felt a familiar lonely ache.

I got to play bridge quite often as time passed and this, too, was fun. Rusty wasn't mad about the game, but Steve loved it. So sometimes he and I would play against various pairs of opponents, while Rusty kibitzed. But attuned as we might be across a card table, I knew where Steve's real interest lay. And Rusty seemed to grow increasingly fond of him.

"Just at first," she confided to me, "I felt he was too inclined to want everyone to like him, that he didn't have enough character to be himself. But that's not true. He's so gentle and sweet, he gives the impression of not being a very positive personality. Actually, he has a lot of inner strength and there are greater depths in him than you realize."

I couldn't agree more. I liked Steve. And seeing Rusty and him getting along so well was a pleasure for me, too.

There were just two things that troubled me during those early weeks in France. The first was that I felt myself to be living in a veritable nest of Americans. I spoke French or heard it spoken, just about as often as when I was taking French conversation back at Park. This was partly my own fault, I knew. When at the movies, I should concentrate more carefully. And I could make a greater effort to talk with French people, not just with Madame and the woman who cleaned our room and the nuns at the convent. The fact that all my classes except one were in English didn't help a bit. And Rusty and I, despite frequent resolutions to speak French to each other, found ourselves slipping as soon as the conversation got interesting and we really wanted to communicate. It would be different, though, in November when the French students arrived, or at least so I kept telling myself.

My other problem was more basic, one that required a definite adjustment, a real change of attitude on my part. Classes and homework didn't nearly occupy all my time. I had begun to suspect I'd never be very pressed with studying. Back at Park, between the harder curriculum and the work program, I used to get up early and be kept very busy all day. Even a fair amount of my evenings had been filled with homework, leaving mostly just week-ends for social stuff. Here things moved much more slowly, which tended just at first to make me feel somewhat tense and nervous. I had the sensation of being half in school and half out of it and an uneasy feeling of guilt dogged me for wasting so much time.

However, as that first month in France slipped away, I became aware of a subtle change in my attitude. It was a little hard for me to describe, even to Rusty, but I tried.

"After years of living by the clock and having a regular schedule, it's as if I suddenly threw the clock away. Just at first I felt rather lost without it," I admitted, "but gradually I seem to be adjusting to the situation. I don't even care anymore. It's strange, but sort of peaceful and relaxing."

Rusty nodded, her brown eyes gleaming. "I know exactly what you mean! It's been happening to me, too—and I like it!"

"Take the matter of meals," I went on. "It no longer bothers me a bit to spend two hours on lunch and two more on dinner."

"And breakfast." Rusty waved a hand at the dishes spread across our desk. We had been eating in our room this week, because they were painting the first floor of the Pavillon. "It used to be a complete blank. I'd get up as late as possible, gulp some orange juice and never really wake up till the middle of my first class. Now I take time to savor every bite. What's happening to us?"

"I guess we're learning to live the French way," I said. Looking back, it seemed to me I had taken my first small step in that direction the day I had walked in the country and been almost equally thrilled by a view of Cézanne's mountain and a friendly greeting from a farmer working his field. I went on, "How did Professor Wencelius put it? Something like 'Enjoy life minute by minute and don't think too much about the hours.' That's the way they do over here and it's beginning to seem like a good idea."

"I know," Rusty agreed. "It just takes time to put on the brakes. Back at Iowa, you didn't think you were living unless you had some sort of date every night and something really big to do on week-ends. I can hardly remember the names of all the fellows I went out with, but I never had time really to know any of them well, to understand what they were like inside."

Rusty, I realized, must have changed as much as I had, maybe even more. We had become good friends during the time we'd been together. We might not have too much in common even yet, still the area in which our interests overlapped seemed to be growing. Both of us had developed the capacity for taking pleasure in simple things, of appreciating the present instead of straining toward the future all the time. Suddenly I was struck by a rather shattering thought. If I had met Rusty in college back home, I would never have taken the time to get to know her at all. We'd have been too different to become friends; neither of us would have thought the other had anything worth while to offer. And yet, having been thrown together by circumstance, in surroundings unfamiliar to us both, we had learned we could enjoy our association very much. And liking and respect had broadened and deepened between us, since it had been given sufficient time to develop.

How many other friends might I have missed, I wondered, through my tendency to catalog some people as just not my type?

The golden October days slipped calmly past. We studied and loafed, played bridge and saw movies, sat around discussing religion and philosophy for hours with other students. We attended an occasional concert or play when a touring company visited the centuries-old theater in Aix. Sometimes Rusty and I went shopping in Marseilles. We had been warned so often about the wickedness of the big, boisterous harbor city, that we scuttled off like a pair of frightened rabbits whenever a sailor, in picturesque pompon cap, so much as glanced at us. But in Aix we felt quite at home and at ease and we continued to absorb the French attitude of enjoying each moment to the fullest. In only one respect were Rusty and I yearning toward the future. We were eager for the French students to arrive. Much as we enjoyed each other's company, we felt it would be more broadening to have a French girl for a roommate.

We were a bit apprehensive when Madame admitted that the French girls who would be living in the Pavillon did not yet know that they were expected to room with Americans.

"But will they do it?" we asked.

Madame shrugged, a typical French shrug, and spread her plump hands appealingly. "You can persuade them," she assured us. "I have no authority in the matter. None whatever."

"Oh, fine," I said to Rusty. "We may end up living together all year after all."

"If I can't have a French girl," Rusty smiled, "you're my next choice. We'll just have to keep our fingers crossed."

After talking with students who lived elsewhere, we felt we were pretty lucky in the Pavillon. True, Madame had tightened up on showers, locking the door except on Wednesdays and Saturdays. And she insisted we hang our washing in the basement laundry room, informing us gravely that it would be very bad for the plaster in our room if we did otherwise. Of course, we continued to hang our wash in our room at night. And our cleaning woman didn't give us away, even though she often caught us with our rubber line still up in the morning. Madame earned our undying gratitude when she turned on the heat in mid-October, rather than waiting till the first of November, as was the inexorable system in other rooming houses. We decided she had done this because the rattle of our teeth probably kept her awake.

On the last Sunday in October, Rusty and I were walking along the Cours Mirabeau on our way back from dinner, when we heard a band playing. Men's voices were raised in rollicking song and suddenly we were surrounded by a crowd of young Frenchmen in medieval costumes. One, on bended knee, vowed his everlasting love for us in ardent French. Then he leaped up and kissed each of us on both cheeks. Before we could catch our breath, four other young men went through the same baffling, but not unenjoyable, routine. A laughing group had gathered about us by the time the Frenchmen blew us an airy kiss and moved on. Bystanders explained that these were engineering students, due to start school the next day and that this was their annual night of celebration and fun.

That was the beginning of our busiest week so far. Madame had asked us to move up to the third floor on Saturday, "just until necessary arrangements can be made for you to have French roommates." By this time we were a bit dubious as to whether this would work out, but we were still hoping. On Thursday night I stayed up quite late, typing a paper for one of the men students who didn't have a typewriter. The next day there was a reception for American Fulbright students who had just arrived to attend the Foreign Students' branch of the University. The Institute students were invited, too, as were a few French students. The reception itself was quite stiff and formal, but some of us congenial souls got together later and went dancing at the University Club, which was most enjoyable. Rusty and I got to bed very late that night, with the prospect of moving the next morning hanging over us.

When we went down to breakfast in the newly decorated lounge, I got the surprise of my life. There was Dave Schultz awaiting me. His grin was as sardonic as ever and the sight of it gave me a nice warm glow. It seemed he had been in Toulon visiting a distant cousin and had decided, being so near, to drop in and see me, too.

The three of us talked like mad over breakfast. Dave told us about Nancy and we told him about Aix. Then we broke the news that we were going to have to move up to the third floor that day.

"How come?" Dave asked.

"Because the French students are arriving and the second floor will be for men, the third for girls," I explained.

"That's a good reason," Dave grinned. "I'll help you."

We were grateful for a strong man when we began transferring all our stuff from one room to another. It took quite a while and, when we were finally all moved in, I apologized. "This wasn't much of a way to entertain you."

"That's okay," Dave said. "At least, I can take you out to dinner. And I don't have to leave till tomorrow afternoon."

The evening passed pleasantly. It was fun to talk with Dave again, to have a real date. "What shall we do tomorrow?" he asked as we were saying goodnight in the Pavillon courtyard.

My tone was rueful, explaining, "I've got a long, long philosophy paper to type. You could have picked a better week-end."

"I'm a mean man with the keys," Dave chuckled. "I'll help."

And he did! In fact, he typed almost the whole paper for me, while I did the rest of my accumulated homework. Then we went for a long walk through the bright fall day, stopping at sidewalk cafés for refreshments, talking and talking about everything imaginable. Dave even undertook to clarify the French educational system for me, when I admitted it had me somewhat baffled.

I knew about the lycée, roughly the equivalent of our high school plus two years of college. Only students who pass a stiff test can get into this. The others must settle for some sort of technical school. Then those who complete the lycée take another tough test, which only about half of them pass. If they make the grade, they get a certificate which entitles them to go on to the university —that is, if they can afford it. Tuition is free, but room and board costs too much for a lot of them. So there are quite a few scholarships and the competition is tough.

"Mr. Maza explained about that," I told Dave, "and how at the end of their first year at the university they have another terrific exam that eliminates a lot more of them."

Dave nodded. "From that point on, they concentrate almost entirely on their major field of study. But there's no discipline as far as attending classes, the professors don't check up on them. But if the students don't read and study all the time, they're in trouble, because there's always a big exam at the end of the term. If they make it through four years, they get a degree that corresponds approximately to our M.A. The only ones who stay in school after that are those who are working toward a still higher degree, so they can be college professors or something of the sort."

"But what I don't get," I told him, "is how the Institute for Foreign Students ties in. It's connected with the University some way, but it's entirely separate from our Institute for American Universities, even though their building is right next door to ours. And students are coming there from all over Europe—Germans, Swiss, Scots, Austrians—"

When I stopped for breath, Dave explained, "Almost all European universities sponsor Institutes for Foreign Students. There are fewer classes, the subjects are broader and lectures are given in simpler language. Foreign students take tests and can earn some sort of certificate. Of course, they could attend classes at the regular university here if they wanted to, just as you're free to. But they can't take exams and earn credit toward a regular French degree, because they haven't gone through the lycée and all the required preliminaries first. Now do you understand?"

"I'm beginning to," I nodded, after a moment's thought. "But it's certainly complicated. Thanks for explaining."

"Any time," Dave grinned at me.

Before he left Aix later that afternoon, we had decided one thing for sure. During the Christmas holidays, he would meet Rusty and me in Italy and the three of us would explore that country together. From what I had heard about Italian men, it might be a very good idea for two young women to have a trusted countryman along when they traveled.

8

THANKSGIVING WITH A DIFFERENCE

Soon after the arrival of the French students, two distressing facts became all too clear. One: my chances of rooming with a French girl were practically nonexistent. And two: at least ninety-five per cent of the Frenchmen were shorter than I.

There was nothing to be done about the second sad situation. But Rusty and I put up quite a struggle against the first. We went out of our way to make friends with the French girls who came to live in the Pavillon; we were as sweet and ingratiating as we knew how to be. And they responded with equal sweetness and friendliness. But when we broached the subject of their moving in with either of us, or letting one of us move in with one of them—well, that was different. They were so sorry, in a sweet and friendly way, but they had already planned to room with Marie, or Lisette, or Lili and they couldn't possibly change. We got some variation of this reaction from everyone we approached and so did the rest of the Americans. Some of the girls were so angry they considered moving out of the Pavillon and finding other living quarters. But this actually wouldn't have helped.

There was no assurance we'd have better luck in another boarding house. And, at least, we were comfortable where we were, which was more than could be said for some of the students who had chosen to live with private families.

Naturally Rusty and I were disappointed. Congenial as we had turned out to be, we both craved the more broadening and enlightening experience of living with a French girl.

Lucy, a vivaciously attractive girl from Marseilles with whom we became quite close friends, couldn't understand this. "But why do you want to change?" she queried. "You have so much more in common than you could possibly have with one of us." And when we had explained, she shook her dark head in wonderment. "It is different with us French. We form little cliques and then develop a sort of inertia about associating with strangers. We don't dislike Americans, but there is a touch of reserve in our relationships with them, because of the difference in our backgrounds, our viewpoints. But you mustn't be hurt by this. It is just our way." Her warm smile flashed. We knew she was honestly trying to be helpful.

"So," I said to Rusty later, "that's the way it is and there's no use banging our heads against a stone wall in our efforts to change it. Right?"

"Right!" Rusty agreed. "Shall we start talking French to each other again?"

"Oui," I nodded.

That time we kept it up for a full day before we began to backslide. But at least we made a point of eating with French students in the University cafeteria, where we had now begun to have our meals. Also, now that the Institute for Foreign Students was in session, I sat in on quite a few lectures there, in addition to my regular required classes. Here, among students of every nationality imaginable, I found little trouble in following the words of the professors, who made an effort to speak French slowly and distinctly for the benefit of us foreigners. It was a definite challenge and my ability to meet it made me more determined than ever to take most of my courses in French the following semester.

Early in November there was a reception for all the foreign students and close to a hundred and fifty turned up. Of this number, about half were German and, to my delight, most of them were not only very friendly, but quite tall. I didn't actually meet anyone who snowed me, but it was such a treat just to be able to look up at a man once more. Afterwards, about thirty of us adjourned en masse to Les Deux Garçons for coffee.

This proved to be only the first of many such "group dates." Quite often a whole crowd of us, Americans, French and Germans, would go out dancing. On these occasions I was just as happy that I was too tall for the French boys. Most of them wanted to dance so close that the short American girls had a bit of a problem. But the tall Germans and Americans were fine to dance with, as relaxed and casually friendly as one could ask. Of course, it wasn't the same as dancing with Brad, but it was so much more fun than those earlier man-less weeks that I wasn't complaining.

We danced in places called The Cave and Moulin d'Huile, picturesque night clubs dripping with atmosphere. We tried all sorts of unusual foods, things we'd never have dreamed of eating back home. Truffles, horsemeat, even snails—everything tasted wonderful in France! Most of the music was by means of hi-fi and the records practically always American. When it happened to be a tune Brad and I had danced to, I felt my heart twist with loneliness for him. Seeing Rusty and Steve dancing happily together made the ache inside of me more intense. Why hadn't I been lucky enough to find a Steve, too, I wondered? Not that I wanted to replace Brad permanently, only while we were far apart. Sometimes my feelings were so mixed up, the yearnings and needs that gnawed at me so intense, I wasn't quite sure what I did want.

With the approach of Thanksgiving, my loneliness shifted away from Brad toward my family. What was I doing away over here in Europe, while the clan would be getting together for our customary big turkey dinner back home? I could almost smell the tantalizing aromas, sense the bustle and excitement that always went on, culminating in the big day itself. And thinking ahead to Christmas, now only a little over a month off, was even worse. I didn't see how I was going to stand that.

Since the Institute was set up on a schedule approximating that of an American college, we learned that we would have four days off over the Thanksgiving weekend, even though that particular holiday meant nothing to the French. Rusty and I, along with Joan Thomas and another American named Nancy Meyers, decided this would be a good time to go to Switzerland. It was common knowledge that the Swiss exchange rate of francs was so much higher than in France that we could pay our train fare out of the money we'd make by cashing our American traveler's checks there. We could leave Marseilles late Wednesday night and reach Geneva the next morning. This would give us three days to see the sights, since we wouldn't have to get back to Aix until Sunday evening.

Wednesday night we were all packed and ready, waiting in the station for the last trolley-bus of the night to take us to Marseilles. According to the schedule, this left at ten-thirty, so along about ten-forty we began to get a little uneasy. Then a man with an official-looking cap came up and informed us that the last bus had gone half an hour earlier. It seemed we had been looking at the Sunday schedule! Naturally we were frantic and, as always in times of dire emergency, our thoughts turned to Mr. Maza. We phoned his home, but he wasn't there. However, when we confided our dilemma to the maid, she told us the name of the café where he and his wife were having a late supper. We rushed off to find him and he left his sympathetic wife finishing her meal while he drove us to Marseilles in his trusty little Dauphine. We made our train with only a few minutes to spare.

We had reserved "couchettes," as the second class sleeping arrangements were called, without having a very clear idea what they were. They proved to be a sort of triple bunk bed deal, six people to a room. We were each given a pillow and a blanket and we all slept in our clothes. There was even one man in our room. But, other than the fact that he snored, he gave us no trouble.

We reached Geneva at eight-thirty of a chill gray morning. In the big, busy station we were greeted by a little lady with red hair and an arm band reading: "For the protection of young girls." It seemed she was affiliated vaguely with the Y.W.C.A., or at least so we gathered. We tried to explain politely that we were quite capable of finding a hotel for ourselves. But our protectress, though pleasant, had certain characteristics in common with a steam-roller. Almost before we knew what was happening, she had phoned to reserve a room for us at a place called "The Foyer," which, she assured us, we would find comfortable, suitable and inexpensive. As for us, we were just a little dubious.

However, The Foyer turned out to be a modern-looking and attractive place. We met our landlady on the fourth floor, where the office was located. From her we learned that only women guests were permitted, that we would have to be in by midnight and that our room, with breakfast, would cost the equivalent of one dollar a day. Naturally, this pleased us, since we wanted to save as much of our money as possible for shopping. So we signed the register, supplied all the additional information always required by European hotels, such as passport number, name of parents, birth date and so on, and were shown up to our room.

Ah, there was the rub! Our room was on the sixth floor, reached by a winding old staircase. It was obviously in the attic, because the ceiling slanted at a sharp pitch. Although the room was large, it and its furnishings were very old. Apparently the face-lifting done on the lower part of the building hadn't extended this far. We had running water—icy in both faucets! The toilet was at least half a block down the hall, with no lights, no paper —luckily we had brought along a roll from Aix! and no heat. Our bedroom was heated a little bit, but not enough to stop our teeth from chattering.

Still, we decided to stay. After all, we'd only be sleeping here and the beds looked comfortable. Moreover, they were well equipped with blankets and had fluffy feather comforters and feather mattresses as well. I hadn't seen a feather mattress since I was a child, visiting a great aunt who lived in the country. But I remembered how toasty warm and snuggly they were.

We lost no time about getting cleaned up and starting our three crowded days of sight-seeing, shopping and, as it turned out, eating! Geneva is a lovely city, sparkling clean and modern. There are beautiful stores, where we proceeded to do most of our Christmas shopping, in addition to buying a generous stock of sweaters for ourselves. Walking along the wide streets, our attention was arrested every few feet by the most tempting delicacies, artfully displayed in the windows of pastry shops. These proved our undoing. We had thought the pastries in Aix couldn't be equaled, but these were even better. Moreover, in France they consider it uncivilized to serve ice cream in the winter. But we could get it in Switzerland, and it was delicious. We took an extensive bus tour of the city and along the shore of the lovely lake that borders it, partly to get our minds off food. There was no point, though, in taking a tour up into the mountains, as we had planned. The clouds were so heavy, we wouldn't have been able to see a thing. This was a disappointment, still it left us more time for Geneva itself.

We ate our Thanksgiving dinner in an Oriental café, where we sat on low chairs in a dim, smoky, crowded room with a great deal of atmosphere and very exotic food. All about us people were talking in French or

German, although we had found that a great many Swiss people spoke excellent English.

"It's not much like Thanksgiving at home," Rusty sighed.

"No turkey or pumpkin pie." I shook my head.

"Stop it," Joan commanded, "or you'll have me crying into whatever this strange concoction is—and I don't think it will improve the flavor!"

She was right. We might all be feeling homesick inside, but there was absolutely no point in getting morbid about it.

The cold in Geneva was bone-chilling all the time we were there. In Aix the temperature hadn't yet dropped below forty, so we weren't acclimated, although luckily we'd brought along our warmest clothes. At night we piled into bed completely dressed, except for skirts and shoes. Our bedroom got so frigid that the only way we could keep our feet warm was to wear knee socks with a pair of bobby socks underneath. But once we were snuggled into our mountains of covers, we felt cozy and comfortable.

We got back to Aix on Sunday afternoon and it was wonderful to feel the warm sunshine again and not to see our own breath preceding us in a white cloud.

Rusty went out with Steve that night and, when she got back, there was a look of enchantment about her.

"Have a nice reunion?" I asked. I had been reading over and answering a long letter from Brad which had come during my absence, so I was feeling rather enchanted myself.

She nodded, flopping down across her bed and staring up at the ceiling. "You know," she said in a small voice,

"I'm getting so fond of that man it scares me."

"What's scary about it?" I queried.

Rusty sat up and locked her arms around her knees and rested her chin on them. "Always before," she admitted, "I've had a sort of—detached feeling about men. Oh, I've liked a lot of them, I've enjoyed their company, we've had fun together. But that was as far as it went, as far as I'd let it go. I never met anyone I wanted to get really involved with emotionally. I couldn't even imagine such a thing. Just a good-night kiss was something of a struggle for me. I never knew what it meant to feel really close to someone, with no urge to draw back, to pull away—" her voice sort of choked. And then she added, low, but very distinctly, "With Steve, it's different."

"You mean you don't mind kissing him?"

"I actually like it," Rusty said in a wondering tone.

"I'd find it more odd if you didn't," I told her. "Steve's a very nice guy. I hope you appreciate him."

"Oh, I do," Rusty said earnestly. "Only—well, the idea that I may be actually starting to fall in love seems so strange to me. I never really thought I'd fall in love with anyone."

"Oh, come on!" I said. "You're human, aren't you? And falling in love is one of the most human things humans do."

"I know." Rusty turned her face sideways a little so that her lovely mahogany hair swung forward against her cheek. She said then, very quickly and almost belligerently, as though she didn't mean to let even her own feelings high-pressure her into anything, "Of course, I haven't really made up my mind yet."

"Of course not," I agreed.

"I'll be around and Steve will be around till next June—more than six whole months. There's plenty of time."

"Sure there is," I nodded.

But I couldn't help thinking that if her feelings continued to reach out toward Steve, if the thing that was starting to develop between them really did turn out to be love, if nothing happened to spoil or change it—well, it would be wonderful! And in my opinion it couldn't happen to two nicer people.

9

A COMPLICATION NAMED DOUG

Back home the period between Thanksgiving and Christmas always seemed much shorter than the calendar indicated. Curiously enough, the same thing happened in France. Of course we all began getting the Christmas spirit considerably ahead of the actual date. Right after Thanksgiving, Rusty and I wrapped and sent off the gifts we had bought for our families and friends. The wrappings were decidedly makeshift, since fancy papers and sparkling ribbon seemed unheard of in Aix. But we hoped the fact that the gifts were a bit out of the ordinary would make up for any deficiency in packaging. I could just see Dad and my brother in their authentic Basque berets. And others on my list should be pleased with cheese and sweaters from Switzerland and dolls and lingerie from France.

I had given the clan strict instructions not to send me any gifts. We had talked it all over before I left and I had pointed out logically that it just wouldn't make sense to send over a lot of stuff that I'd only have to pack into my already bursting luggage and bring home again. The sensible thing, I had persuaded them, would be to send me a check, with which I could buy something exotic for myself in Europe. The check arrived all right, well ahead of time. But with it was a card on which my mother had written three small apologetic words: "Box on way." If that wasn't just like them, I thought.

The Mazas, sensing that this was the season when virulent homesickness might well attack, began a pleasant ritual of having a get-together for the Institute students every Saturday afternoon. Mrs. Maza served coffee and soft drinks and little cakes and we all sat around in the relaxed atmosphere of their apartment, talking and listening to music. As the holidays drew near, we enjoyed Christmas carols on the record player. And one Saturday, Mr. Maza provided a special treat. With great ceremony he brought out a big jar of peanut butter, which is practically unprocurable in France. Spread on little crackers, nothing ever tasted quite so good to a drooling bunch of expatriates.

In mid-December the Institute for Foreign Students gave its annual Christmas party and we Americans were invited. It was held in a large room in the fanciest restaurant in Aix and some two hundred people were there. After a gay buffet supper, there was a program consisting of carol singing. Each student group sang in its own language and there were many nationalities represented, German, Dutch, Scandinavian, English, French and American. Then we all stood up, the lights were put out except for the candles on the long tables, and everyone sang "Silent Night" in his own language. As all the young voices rose in intermingled tongues, but each following the sweet old tune that seems so much a part of Christmas, a spirit of brotherhood drew us all together in a warm closeness that I hoped would never be broken.

A few days later we Americans had our own Christmas party at the Institute. Things started out rather slowly, since everyone was feeling a little low over being so far away from home. Then someone had the bright idea of combining our efforts to decorate the Institute, or at least the lower floor and the stairs leading to Mr. Maza's office. What a ball that was! We strung holly and pine branches all over, put up improvised ornaments and big bows of red ribbon and drew Christmas pictures on all the blackboards. For a while we played carols on the record player, but that made us feel too nostalgic, so we switched to dance music. We danced till Mr. Maza told us regretfully he had to close up the place. Then we walked home arm in arm, in laughing twos and threes, our footsteps echoing on the pavements in the midnight stillness of the sleeping town.

Our packages arrived from home, but Rusty and I decided to wait to open them until the evening before we were going to leave for Venice. In the meantime, I concocted a tree out of a Coke bottle wrapped in a dark green towel and this we trimmed with Kleenex snowballs and ornaments contrived from the gold and silver paper that cheese comes in. We stacked our gaily wrapped gifts around it and the effect was quite festive.

Naturally we were pretty excited about going to Italy for the holidays. Our itinerary was all planned, Venice first, then Florence, Rome, Naples, Capri, any other fascinating place we could possibly crowd into two weeks. Dave, who couldn't get away from college as early as we could, was going to meet us in Rome. But Rusty and I weren't really worried about traveling without a man. Our self-reliance had grown a lot since that distant day when we boarded a plane for New York.

We planned to leave France on the twenty-first of December, which fell on Sunday. That final week of classes progressed quietly enough until Friday afternoon, when Rusty became involved in quite a situation. During the preceding weeks, she had received a couple of letters from a Navy ensign named Doug Manning, who knew some relatives of hers back in Iowa. He had written that his ship would dock in Nice, less than a two-hour trip from Aix, and had asked if he might come to see her on his pass this week-end. And Rusty, knowing that Steve was planning to leave Friday afternoon for Germany, where he'd spend the holidays with his family, had agreed. But Steve, on a sudden impulse, decided to wait until Sunday morning to go home. So when Doug, tall, blond and beaming expectantly, arrived at the Pavillon soon after lunch on Friday, Rusty was really on a spot. Babbling something about having to fix her face, she dragged me up to our room, while Doug waited in the lounge.

"You've got to help me," she begged. "If I go out with Doug tonight, Steve will flip. You know that!"

I did indeed. Some of Steve's friends had him half-persuaded that Rusty was just dating him because there wasn't anyone better around. His suspicion that her interest in him was only a temporary thing wasn't justified, I felt sure. But if she passed up a date with him to go out with a man she scarcely knew, it would surely add fuel to the flame.

"On the other hand," Rusty went on unhappily, "if I brush Doug off after telling him he could come—well, that would be a pretty low blow to a nice guy far away from home."

"Yes, it would," I nodded. "What do you want me to do?"

Her answer was exactly what I'd hoped for. "Let's try to get the whole crowd to go dancing tonight. That way it's hard to tell who's with whom anyway. And if you'll just take Doug off my hands, I'll be everlastingly grateful."

"Well, sure," I agreed delightedly. "That is, if it's all right with him."

Ten of us went to the Moulin d'Huile that night. And the ensign and I got along beautifully. I'm sure he suspected what the situation was with Rusty and Steve. But it was quite flattering to find him undismayed over the switch. In fact, we had so much fun together that he asked me for a date the next night, too. We decided to double with Rusty and Steve and, as things worked out, we spent the greater part of that whole Saturday together. The four of us had lunch at La Taverne, then walked around for a while before settling down to pastries and conversation at our favorite sidewalk café. The weather was still crisp and clear, not cold at all. The great trees along the Cours Mirabeau were leafless now and sunshine fell brightly through their bare branches. It didn't seem possible that Christmas was only five days off.

That night while we dressed to go out, Rusty and I opened our gifts. I should have known I could trust my family's good sense in selecting things to send me. Lingerie and stockings might well wear out before I went home. Stationery I could never get too much of. Films could be put to good use capturing the essence of the places I saw and wanted to remember. And as for the rest—well, what could be more heart-warmingly American in a foreign land than a new Pogo book and a generous carton of Life Savers?

After dinner with Steve and Doug, we saw a very good play in French, which we had to keep translating for Doug's bewildered benefit. The theater where the performance was given was built in sixteen hundred and something and restored in the eighteen-thirties. When you lived in Aix, you grew accustomed to everything being so old. But Doug was very impressed.

"It's safe, isn't it?" he asked a shade apprehensively, glancing up at the overhanging balcony above our heads.

By the time we got back to the Pavillon, it was quite late. We lingered in the chill moonlight of the courtyard, saying our good-byes. I hated to see Doug go, although both of us knew there was nothing lasting between us. But we'd had fun together and each of us, I suspected, had filled a need for the other. It was much harder, I knew, for Rusty to bid Steve good-bye, even though she'd be seeing him again in a couple of weeks.

Later, as we got sleepily ready for bed, Rusty sighed. "I'm going to miss that man," she admitted ruefully.

"I'll bet you are," I agreed. "But think how much fun it'll be, getting together again." I exclaimed then, struck by a sudden thought, "Hey! Do you realize we haven't packed yet?"

"Please," Rusty yawned widely. "We can leave that till morning. The ten o'clock bus will get us to Marseilles in plenty of time for our train."

"I know," I nodded. Actually, it would get us there almost an hour ahead of train time. But the man we had consulted at American Express had warned that we'd better be early, or we might not get seats. "I guess I'd better set the alarm, though."

Rusty climbed into bed and pulled the covers up around her shoulders. "Might be a good idea—but not *too* early."

"Seven o'clock," I said firmly, reaching for my little clock. Rusty moaned, but I ignored her. "That won't be a bit too soon," I said, "by the time we pack and dress and have breakfast and get to the station."

"Ummmmm," was Rusty's only comment.

I wound the clock and set the alarm hand for seven, then turned off the lights and got into bed. It didn't take me long to fall asleep. I was dead tired from all our extra activities of the past few days. And a pleasant mixture of Brad and Doug and all the fun things I'd been doing and the gifts I'd received and the exciting prospect of tomorrow's trip moved dreamily past my mind's eye. I was so enthralled with my last waking thoughts and the cozy warmth and softness of my bed, that I didn't remember having failed to pull out the little thingamajig that made my clock's alarm go off.

10

TRAVEL IS SO BROADENING

I awoke slowly, with that luxurious sense of well-being which follows a good night's sleep. Sunshine poured in between our green curtains and fell warmly and pleasantly across my bed. Suddenly I sat bolt upright as memory flooded over me. I shouldn't have been waking up in such leisurely fashion. I should have been yanked unceremoniously from slumber by the unrelenting ring of my alarm clock. Appalled, I glanced toward the desk where that traitorous mechanical monster stood. *It was five minutes till nine.*

My shriek and the sharp thud of my feet hitting the floor should have aroused Rusty. But they didn't—not Rusty! She could sleep through anything. I fell upon her mercilessly, dragging the covers off, shaking and pummeling her shrinking form till she finally awakened.

"It's late!" I yelled. "Terribly late! You've got to get right up. We'll never get packed and ready if you don't. Hurry!"

"What happened?" Rusty yawned, struggling to a sitting position and rubbing her eyes.

"Something went wrong with the blasted clock," I

told her. I hadn't yet checked and found it was my own absent-mindedness which had brought us to this sorry situation. "Get up!"

Rusty got. Still in my pjs, I packed our suitcase while she dressed, so that we wouldn't get in each other's way at the lavatory and closet. We had decided that one large bag would hold all our clothes for the two-week trip. Luggage is such a nuisance when you have too much of it, that we both preferred to travel light. By the time Rusty was dressed, I had finished packing. Then, while I got ready, she gathered up the supply of food we had acquired for our lunch on the train. What a change had taken place in our thinking since that initial trip of ours across France, when we had considered it queer for people to carry their food along. Now such a course was second nature to us.

We left our room in a state of indescribable confusion, beds unmade, clothes scattered everywhere, and rushed downstairs at fifteen minutes till ten. We grabbed a few hasty bites of breakfast, bid the other people in the lounge good-bye and lit out for the bus station, each of us eating a piece of bread as we hurried along. When we arrived, we found we had five whole minutes to spare—quite an accomplishment, everything considered. We also found Doug awaiting us. He had decided to take the same bus and train we did, instead of a later one as he had originally planned. I felt very sheltered and taken care of when his hand gripped the handle of the suitcase I'd been carrying, also flattered to realize he wanted to be with me as long as possible.

We discovered that four other Institute students would be traveling with us for a while. So we had lots of company to start out with and, due to our early arrival at the railway station in Marseilles, we were able to share a compartment. It turned out that all of us had brought food along, so we pooled our cheese, bread, fruit, cookies, potato chips and wine, and had quite a lunch!

Everyone was in a gay mood and time passed quickly. We were enthralled by lovely brief glimpses of the French Riviera caught as our train flashed past. The Mediterranean was incredibly blue and calm in the sunshine and pastel-colored villas perched on the hills above it, with lush flowers cascading down their walls. Doug left us at Nice to rejoin his ship and, once again, I hated to see him go. This time it was really for keeps.

Rusty and I were the next to leave the crowd. We got off the train late in the afternoon at the town of Ventimiglia, just across the French-Italian border. You pronounce it, we discovered, as though that g isn't even there. We went through customs, a routine business consisting mainly of the checking of our passports—you'd really be in a bad way without your passport anywhere in Europe—and polite inquiries as to where we planned to go in Italy and how long we intended to remain. All the time we were involved with the customs official, Rusty was devoting part of her attention to cleaning a large blob of soft cheese off the front of her lovely new black leather coat. The string bag in which she was carrying our left-over food had betrayed her. By the time she discovered that some fruit had crushed the cheese out of its wrappings, the damage had been done. We threw the cheese away, but cleaning off the resultant mess was quite a job, which made Rusty a bit slow in answering some of the official's questions. Eventually, though, we were finished with all the border red tape.

Not until then did we learn that the Venice train was due to leave in five minutes. We made a mad dash for the ticket window, but, of course, there were several excitable Italians in line ahead of us, all buying tickets for distant points, which required a great deal of discussion. Result, we missed our train.

After that, we relaxed and enjoyed the upheaval until it was finally our turn to talk to the ticket agent. He spoke only a very little French and no English. We spoke no Italian. This complicated matters. I tried to explain that what we wanted to buy was a special tourist ticket, second-class, which we had been told about at the American Express office in Marseilles. This was supposed to cost fifteen thousand lire, a mere twenty-four dollars in American money, and could be used for train travel anywhere in Italy for fifteen days. All the time I was describing it, the ticket seller stared admiringly, first at Rusty, then at me. When I had finished, he spread his hands helplessly, shook his head and launched into a regretful stream of Italian. Obviously, he didn't have the vaguest idea what I was talking about.

However, he directed us to an office where I launched into another long explanation, this time for a man who, luckily, understood French. At first, he, too, seemed puzzled. Then a great light broke over him and he began to nod excitedly. Now, I thought, we're getting somewhere!

"Oh, yes!" the man exclaimed, nodding and beaming. "I understand. I know exactly the ticket you mean."

Suddenly his pleased expression faded, like the sun being blotted out by a cloud. "However," he went on, his tone matching his altered look, "you can purchase those only at travel bureaus, not in railway stations." His face grew even more doleful and his voice assumed a still sadder note as he added, "And all travel bureaus are closed today, because it's Sunday."

"But what will we do?" Rusty and I exclaimed, practically in unison. And we both looked as helpless and forlorn as possible, my green eyes and Rusty's brown ones clinging beseechingly to the poor man's troubled face.

"Don't be alarmed," he soothed, all his chivalrous Latin instincts rushing to the fore. "Maybe something can be done. I will try my best to help you, that you may depend on! Come back in half an hour."

We thanked him and went out and fooled around the station, looking at travel posters, watching the people coming and going, discussing our dilemma. Of course, we could buy a regular ticket as far as Venice and then pick up the tourist ticket tomorrow. But that would cost extra money and we were both determined to spend as little as possible on anything but clothes and pleasure while in Italy. Keeping travel expenses low had become a sort of game with us ever since we'd got to Europe. And we had no intention of starting to throw money around like a pair of Americans now.

When we returned to our new-found friend's office, we discovered that he hadn't failed us. He had gone out and rounded up a travel bureau official. The man had been happily drinking wine in a nearby tavern with a group of friends, but upon hearing of our sad plight, his heart had been touched. He now proceeded to sell us our tourist tickets. We gave him a tip of a thousand lire, which he seemed to appreciate deeply. Then, thanking both our benefactors, we went out into the station to check on the next train to Venice.

Even the news that we would have to wait until eight-thirty for this failed to dampen our spirits. We frittered away the next three hours people-watching, talking, eating our left-over fruit and nursing two cups of tea for an unbelievable length of time in the station restaurant. If we had learned nothing else in Europe, Rusty and I agreed, we surely had discovered the secret of how to waste time enjoyably.

When our train pulled in, we discovered that the cars for Milan, where we would have to make a change, were almost empty. We found a second-class compartment all to ourselves and decided to stretch out and get some sleep. The two wooden seats were hard, but each was long enough to accommodate four people. We took our towels from the suitcase, wrapped them in plastic sweater-bags for cleanliness and used them for pillows. We even set my alarm clock so we'd be sure not to miss Milan at five-thirty in the morning.

Scarcely were we all settled when we stopped at a station where many people boarded the train. We could hear their voices and footsteps, but we had turned out our light, closed the door and pulled the curtain of our compartment. And no one tried to get in. I know, because I was holding the doorknob, just in case.

We were almost asleep when the conductor came for our tickets. He was young, nice and cute in a little-boy sort of way. He spoke fair French and stayed there talking to us for quite some time. We pretended to be French, because it's such fun to fool people, and his understanding of the language wasn't sufficient for him to know the difference. He was very impressed with the manner in which we had made ourselves at home. He apologized abjectly for the hardness of the seats and even offered to smuggle us up to a first-class compartment, where the seats were padded. But we didn't think we'd better take advantage of his kind offer. How could we be sure some other, less accommodating conductor might not have charge of things up there? Besides, we were too comfortable to move.

After the friendly conductor had gone, we slept fairly soundly for several hours. Whenever the train stopped and new passengers approached and started to open our door, I'd discourage them with, "*C'est prise, monsieur,*" meaning, "It's taken, sir." Since "prise" means the same thing in Italian, this did the trick. Of course, the fact that our light was out and the curtain drawn helped, too. No one could see that only two of us were occupying the whole compartment. And I made my voice sound quite firm and authoritative, knowing the conductor was on our side. So all intruders excused themselves and went and sat elsewhere.

However, our little game was up when two old peasant women opened our door and peered in suspiciously. My words of warning had no effect on them; they advanced like a pair of bulldozers, addressing us in reproachful Italian. We couldn't understand their language, but their gestures made it quite clear that they had no intention of letting us sleep stretched out like that, taking up all that space. I imagine they were telling us we should be ashamed of ourselves. They sat down determinedly, one on each seat, beside each one of us. And before we realized what was happening, they had proceeded to stretch out comfortably and go off to sleep themselves, leaving us hardly room to sit! In a way, I suppose it was ironic justice. Luckily for us, though, they only rode a couple of hours. And after they left, we got away with sweet and uninterrupted slumber until five-thirty, when the alarm went off.

Our friend the conductor helped us solicitously from the train in Milan, his dark young glance embarrassingly direct and admiring. Staring admiringly at women seems to be the favorite sport of Italian men. We'd been warned about that by other students who had traveled in Italy, so I guessed we'd just have to get used to it. After breakfast in the station, we boarded our train for Venice.

Staring through the window at the gray, overcast morning, Rusty brooded, "Why do they call it sunny Italy, I wonder?"

"Don't give up yet," I said. "It wouldn't dare rain in Venice. Whoever heard of such a thing?"

This train was quite crowded, still we dozed, sitting bolt upright. It was so early yet and there was something sleep-inducing about the cloudy weather, the rather stuffy warmth of our compartment and the buzz of voices all about us, speaking a language we couldn't understand. After a little time, though, our drowsiness passed and Rusty and I began talking.

We spoke in French, continuing our earlier innocent pretense that we were natives of that country. Several surprised looks flashed our way. But the astonishment we caused was short-lived and not nearly so great as it would have been had we spoken in English. However, there was one quite attractive Italian man sitting opposite us, who had been staring before we began talking and who continued to do so quite unabashedly, his warmly appreciative glance scarcely leaving our faces.

After an hour or so of this, we began talking about him.

"Isn't it queer," I asked Rusty in French, "how they can stare like that without the slightest embarrassment?"

Rusty nodded. "They look at you as though you were the first girl they ever saw and they didn't want to miss a single detail. What do you suppose he'd do if I made a face at him?"

"Don't you dare!" I had to grin at the thought of the pained look of surprise with which he'd react to such treatment.

"Oh, I won't," Rusty said. "But I wish he'd look out the window for a while. He makes me self-conscious."

"He's rather cute, don't you think?" I queried.

"Um-hum," Rusty admitted. "Reminds me of Dean Martin, only much older."

"He's probably married and has half a dozen children."

"Oh, at least," Rusty smiled.

After that we got to talking about school and tried not to look at the man opposite. Whenever we did glance his way, though, his gaze was fixed unwaveringly on us. As the train neared Venice, he rose to take down his bag from the luggage rack overhead. "Is this one yours?" he asked us in flawless French.

Rusty blushed crimson and I could feel hot color

creeping across my face, too, as I gulped, "*Oui—merci—*"

A faint smile curved his lips as he set our heavy suitcase down in front of us. Graciously he acknowledged our mumbled thanks. But the final blow fell when he glanced at the name-tag on our bag and said, as though that explained everything, "Ah, Americans!"

11

WHEN IN VENICE

The sun had begun to shine brightly by the time we emerged from the railway station and embarked on our search for a suitable place to stay. "You see?" I told Rusty. "I knew it couldn't rain in Venice. It just wouldn't be fitting."

"I hope you're right." Her tone was a shade dubious.

Venice, as everyone knows, is an extremely old city built on a large group of islands in the Adriatic Sea. Why such a site was chosen, even for a city originally engaged in the shipping business, is a bit hard to grasp. However, there it has been for well over a thousand years and it still looks amazingly solid, all things considered. The huge, ornate buildings, many of them actual palaces, are set on piles, their broad, rather moldy-looking stone steps going right down into the water. Most of the principal streets are waterways and more than a hundred and seventy-five smaller canals connect with the Grand Canal, which you might say is Venice's Main Street. Of course, there are many stone-paved thoroughfares, too, along which one can walk. But there are no cars, no trucks or buses. Transportation is handled by picturesque gondolas, bustling motor launches and a number of large motorized vessels, capable of carrying forty or fifty passengers, which Rusty and I came to call affectionately "commuter boats." These ply their way back and forth along the main canals, keeping a regular schedule and making frequent stops, just as if they were buses or streetcars.

Of course, the railway station is on solid ground, as are many other buildings nearby, including the huge Car-Park where people traveling by auto must leave their cars before going into the city proper. Rusty and I decided to look for a pension, or boarding house, in this neighborhood, since it seemed quite convenient.

We found a nice-looking place only a few blocks from the station. Fairly new, as Venetian buildings went, it was very clean and inviting. A fat, cheerful landlady who spoke a little French, showed us a room with its own balcony overlooking the bright, busy street. It was warm and cozy, there was hot water available at the lavatory opposite the beds, and a spotlessly clean bathroom just down the hall. Naturally, we were delighted.

"How much is it?" I asked a trifle fearfully.

"Eleven hundred lire apiece," the landlady said.

We consulted our currency converter and stared at each other unbelievingly. That was only a dollar seventy-five in American money. Yet we had been told in advance that the Italians love to bargain, that they never remotely expect to be paid the first price they ask for anything. Her rate sounded most reasonable, still one had to play the game according to the rules, I supposed.

So I said doubtfully, "That's too much, I'm afraid."

And Rusty fixed her limpid brown eyes on the woman's face and said gently, "We're students, you see."

"Ah, students." The woman nodded understandingly. Then, with a beaming smile, she said, "Nine hundred lire to you."

We bargained back and forth enthusiastically for a while, all enjoying ourselves thoroughly. Eventually we got the room for seven hundred lire, or a dollar and ten cents apiece. Including breakfast, of course. European accommodations almost always include breakfast. The landlady patted our shoulders with warm affection as she left. I had the feeling she wouldn't have liked us nearly as well if we had simply paid the first price she named. Then she could have been haunted by the suspicion that we'd have paid even more if she'd asked for it. This way, she respected our level heads and could feel helpful and generous. Everyone was happier all around. I decided I could learn to like this bargaining bit.

That first afternoon in Venice we bought a map of the city and with it in hand started out for St. Mark's Square and the inevitable American Express office, without which American travelers in Europe would be sunk. We took the commuter boat part way and were entranced with the colorful activity of the Grand Canal. Graceful gondolas glided along, propelled by darkly handsome boatmen in their traditional white blouses and straw sailor hats, with streamers hanging down in back. Faster moving launches zipped in and out. And both gondolas and launches carried, not only people, but every imaginable type of cargo, from fruit and vegetables to mortar and bricks and lumber for new construction or repair. We passed towering ancient palaces with extravagantly ornamented façades and glimpsed intriguing narrow canals that led off on every side, like leaf-veins branching from the main stem.

Finally we disembarked at a landing which we judged wasn't too far from the famous square we were seeking. We wandered along happily, entranced by shop windows where fabulous Venetian glass and tooled leather and lovely shoes and clothing were displayed. We climbed over little arched bridges that crossed the canals, then couldn't resist pausing to stare down into the dark water that flowed so slowly beneath, making soft gurgling noises against the buildings. Before long, despite our map, we were hopelessly lost. All the narrow streets looked alike and our sense of direction had grown confused with our twistings and turnings.

A handsome, well-dressed woman, accompanied by a girl of twelve or so, seemed a safe enough person of whom to ask directions. She obviously didn't understand French, or English, but when I said inquiringly, "San Marco?" and pointed it out on our map, she smiled and nodded. Moreover, she insisted on sending her child along with us to show us the way.

We thanked her and followed the young Italian girl for blocks and blocks and blocks! By the time we reached St. Mark's we felt horribly guilty over taking her so far out of her way. But she waved aside our offer of a few hundred lire. However, when I found a couple of packages of Life Savers in my purse, she accepted these with obvious delight.

"Imagine being that helpful!" Rusty exclaimed as we waved good-bye to the child.

"Do you suppose all Italians are like that?" I wondered.

"Time will tell," Rusty grinned. "I have a hunch we're likely to get lost fairly often."

We didn't have time that day to do too much exploring. St. Mark's is a huge square, with marvelous shops on three sides and the great brooding Basilica of St. Mark on the other. Off to the east we could see the enormous white Palace of the Doges and beyond it the blue waters of the Bay of Venice. There are several sidewalk cafés, with orchestras playing from small raised bandstands. And everywhere, circling and wheeling and approaching tamely to light on people's heads or shoulders and eat from their hands, are the pigeons for which the square is famous.

We located the American Express office only a short distance from St. Mark's and here, to our delight, we found a lot of mail awaiting us. I had two letters from Brad and a great fat one from my parents. This, I knew, was the Christmas letter they had promised me and which I must wait to open until Christmas Eve. My heart swelled at the sight of it, aware as I was that it contained messages from all the clan and detailed accounts of their holiday preparations. Standing there with the letter in my hand, I seemed to feel them all hovering near, their affection reaching out to envelop me in spite of the distance between us. I got all choked up and might have burst into tears if there hadn't been so many people milling around. Brad's letters helped, too. There was no reason to wait two days before opening them.

Rusty and I sat right down in the American Express

office to read our mail. Brad's letters were wonderful, as always. They made me ache with loneliness for him, but there was consolation in knowing he missed me, too, and that I wasn't the only one who was counting the months till we'd be together again.

It was dusk by the time we reached the street. By back-tracking we managed to find the commuter boat landing without any trouble. We ate dinner at a restaurant near our pension and discovered, upon reaching our room, that we were both exhausted. This was no wonder, really, considering our fitful sleep on the train the night before. And we had practically walked our feet off since reaching Venice.

"Shall I set the alarm?" I asked when we were ready to get into bed.

"Oh, don't," Rusty yawned. "It's only ten o'clock. We'll be sure to wake up early."

I nodded in agreement and turned out the light. For once we were too tired to lie talking after we'd got into bed.

I've never felt better than when I awoke the next day —that is, until I glanced at the clock and discovered it was practically noon! In spite of the hour, half-darkness lay all about. A trip to the window showed me a gray, miserable day and rain dripping steadily down the glass.

"Sunny Italy, hah!" was Rusty's comment when she joined me. "I'd go back to bed, except that I'm too hungry."

After a breakfast filling enough to be considered brunch, we donned our raincoats and set out for St. Mark's again. The commuter boat wasn't so crowded today, still there were a lot of people besides us riding it. We ducked in and out of doorways and paused to catch our breath under shop awnings on our way to the square. Luckily the shops around St. Mark's are sheltered by a sort of covered arcade, so the weather didn't bother us too much. Eventually it stopped raining, although the sky remained gray and overcast. By the time we got around to checking on guided tours, we learned we were too late to take one that afternoon.

"Let's plan on the nine o'clock tour in the morning," I suggested. "If we don't walk around all the points of interest with a guide, we may miss a lot."

Rusty agreed, so we spent the rest of that day loitering about St. Mark's. We saw the government man come out with his regular supply of food for the pigeons. In some inexplicable way, the birds anticipate the time of his arrival and perch, waiting and ready, on the cornices of the buildings until the gong sounds and he puts in an appearance. Then the whole square grows black as they descend upon it for their free meal. We saw, too, the ancient clock tower, where life-sized mechanical figures move majestically to strike the hour.

By dinnertime our feet ached with so much walking, but we weren't a bit tired otherwise. We found a restaurant that specialized in pizza, which made us feel a little homesick, although we both knew the dish had originated in Italy. After a delicious dinner, we started looking around for an interesting movie. We sat through a German picture, with Italian sound dubbed in, all quite unintelligible to us. Still, it was fun trying to follow the complicated plot without benefit of dialogue. And a kiss means a happy ending in any language, we decided.

"Only one more day and night in Venice," I remarked as we lay talking in bed later.

"Ummmm," Rusty agreed. "Romantic place, isn't it?"

"Sure is," I sighed. "If only Brad were here—"

"And Steve," Rusty added, sighing, too . . .

We were up early the next morning. Our first look out the window showed us another gray, cloudy day, but at least it wasn't raining. "Look at that man down there." I pointed him out to Rusty. "He's barefooted, carrying his shoes."

"Must be nuts," Rusty laughed, "or else planning to go wading in the canal."

Not until we had eaten breakfast and reached the street ourselves did we learn the reason for the poor man's eccentric conduct. All the streets around were flooded, some to a depth of only a few inches, others up to a foot or more. While we stood there, appalled in the doorway, our landlady joined us for a disgusted look at the street. In her limited French, she explained that this sort of thing occasionally happened in the fall, hardly ever in December. It was due, she maintained, to the change of the moon, which resulted in unusually high tides.

"But what can we do?" I asked. "How can we get anywhere?"

The woman indicated a small cart being pushed along the flooded street by a couple of high-booted men, who seemed in the gayest of spirits. In the cart stood half a dozen dignified-looking businessmen, who didn't seem nearly as happy.

"Ride in—that, you mean?" Rusty gulped, as the

booted ones brought their vehicle to a stop beside us.

Our landlady nodded, beaming. "Only to the boat landing."

The businessmen moved over to make room for us, one of the booted ones put out a big hairy hand to help us into the cart. I looked at Rusty and grinned.

"When in Rome," I said, "you're supposed to do as the Romans do. I suppose that goes for Venice as well."

Rusty nodded. "At least, it's better than wading."

The landing was less than a block away, but it seemed farther as we were bounced over the uneven pavement in that rickety cart. However, we didn't get dumped out, our feet stayed dry and the trip cost us only a hundred lire, or sixteen cents.

"Besides," I said to Rusty, "think of the experience!"

On the commuter boat we checked with the helmsman and learned that there was a stop much nearer St. Mark's than the one we had supposed was nearest. Moreover, the streets we had to traverse on foot to get there were almost dry, except for occasional puddles quite easily avoided.

We reached the square in good time, only to be stopped dead in our tracks by a sight we certainly hadn't expected. The entire area was under water, to a depth of what looked like a foot or two! Not only that, we had approached our objective from the wrong direction. The spot from which our intended tour was scheduled to start was on the opposite side, a good block across the sheet of water from where we stood.

12

'TWAS THE NIGHT BEFORE CHRISTMAS

"Now what?" Rusty said, as we stared in blank dismay at the flooded square before us.

Some grimy-looking men were carrying people across. One approached and offered to carry us for fifty lire apiece. It wasn't the money that stopped us. I felt a shiver of revulsion at the leering look the man gave us. And Rusty's expression indicated plainly that she didn't like the idea, either.

"Let's try going around on some back streets and coming in from the opposite direction," I suggested. As we turned and departed hastily, our would-be benefactor called something after us, which it was probably just as well we didn't understand.

We followed a fairly passable street to a small park, where we saw several people climbing over a low stone wall. We watched them make their way from gondola to gondola across a narrow canal and reach the other side safely. There it appeared quite dry.

"Shall we try it?" I asked Rusty.

"Our skirts are pretty tight," she said dubiously, "but I'm game if you are."

The wall was a bit hard to negotiate, but we made it. Then three nice gondoliers, who were keeping their boats close together to form a sort of bridge, were most helpful. Each of them passed us on to the next with a firm hand, so we reached the other side without the slightest trouble. From there it was a simple matter to get to the starting point of our tour. However, a regretful guide was waiting there to inform prospective clients that the tour had been canceled, because too many streets were flooded!

Luckily, good old American Express was close at hand. We sat in the office talking for two hours, waiting for the tide to recede. By eleven o'clock the water had gone down sufficiently so that we were able to go and see glass blowers at work and also a lace-making plant in operation. Both of these were so fascinating, we felt our morning hadn't been wasted after all. We had another pizza for lunch and then went through the Basilica of St. Mark, a very ornate and impressive place, but rather dark and forbidding. By that time the square was dry and our adventures of the early morning assumed a strange, almost dreamlike unreality.

"Do you suppose they get used to this sort of thing here?" Rusty asked.

"Confucius say," I answered, " 'People who build city on a bunch of islands shouldn't mind wet feet.' "

The next thing on our agenda was the Doges' Palace, which we had seen, so far, only from the outside. The interior proved quite gorgeous, with many works of art and sculpture to occupy our attention. It had been built in the fourteenth century and strongly reflected the Byzantine influence, evident in so much of the Venetian architecture and decoration. Out in the street once more, we stood discussing what point of interest to take in next.

" 'Ave you see da Whispering Bridge?" a male voice asked in English and we both jumped with surprise.

A stocky curly-haired gondolier of about thirty lounged nearby, his gondola bobbing lazily in the canal a few feet beyond him. His smile broadened at our evident astonishment and he said, "Americans, no?" At our baffled nods, he added, "I can tell."

"How?" we demanded in unison.

His shrug was eloquent. "Da English sound—diff'-rent."

"They do, at that," I had to admit, laughing.

He wasn't a wolf type at all, just casual and friendly. And it was such a treat to hear our native language spoken, even with an unmistakable Italian accent. Rusty must have felt as I did, because she didn't try to discourage him, either.

"You speak English very well," she told him. "How did you learn it?"

Again the expressive shrug, the wide, white-toothed grin. He had an uncle, he explained, who had lived for years in the United States, before coming back home to Venice. He had taught him some English. "In my gondola," he reached out to touch the tall graceful prow of his boat affectionately, "I learn more. Summertime I 'ave many American passengair. Dey talk, I lissen. If I say somet'ing American, dey amuse. Dey pay more, give bigger tip. Is—how you say?—good biz-niz."

He was so frank, so engaging, we had to laugh.

"Where is the Whispering Bridge you mentioned?" I asked.

"Right over dere," he pointed. "Wait, I go wit' you."

This was a bit more than we'd expected, still he was so very nice and it was broad daylight and there were two of us. He showed us the bridge as proudly as if he'd built it with his own hands and told us its history. Then he said, beckoning us on with an uplifted finger, "Come, I show you somet'ing else."

"We really have to be getting along—" I began.

And Rusty said, "Should you leave your gondola so long? What if some passengers—"

He shook his dark head decisively. "Is no passengair today—da day before Christmas. Don' worry. Look, you mus' see dis." He had crossed the narrow sidewalk and was holding open the door of a small restaurant. We knew it was a restaurant because the sign above the door said "Ristorante," which was too similar to the American word for anyone to make a mistake about it.

"Maybe it's just a come on," Rusty whispered, "to get us to buy him something to eat. But I don't mind, do you?"

I shook my head and together we followed our gondolier friend through the doorway. Just inside the café we stopped to stare unbelievingly at the lovely sight before us. I heard Rusty give a little gasp of pleasure—or had the involuntary sound come from me?

There in the empty restaurant, amid all the white-covered tables, was a real honest-to-goodness Christmas tree, complete with tinsel and ornaments and glittering colored lights! Such a beautiful sight we certainly hadn't expected and the experience left both of us breathless and dazzled for a moment.

"You like it? Is pretty, no?" the gondolier pressed.

"It's lovely," I said softly.

And Rusty murmured, her voice unsteady, "Just like home."

The gondolier called out something in Italian and a moment later a door at the back of the room opened and the proprietor of the place, along with his cheerful pink-cheeked wife and a couple of bright-eyed children came rushing in to welcome us. Of course, they couldn't understand a word we said, any more than we could understand them. But their attitude was so friendly, you couldn't mistake their intentions. And our gondolier acted as interpreter. He told them how beautiful we thought their tree was and they all beamed and nodded happily. Then, after a torrent of Italian, he told us that the proprietor and his wife had said we ought to come there for Christmas Eve dinner that night, that they would be proud and happy to serve us along with the many other holiday merry-makers they expected.

"It does sound like fun, doesn't it?" Rusty murmured, the lights from the tree making her eyes glow.

I nodded, smiling. "Maybe we can come. I'd like to."

When we had thanked them and were outside in the street, our gondolier asked, "Will you eat dere tonight? I'll be dere, too."

He sounded so pleased, I hated to throw cold water on the scheme. Still, I didn't like to rush into anything. "We'll see," I hedged. "Don't count on it, though."

We walked back along the way we had come and when we reached the spot where he had left his gondola, he informed us, "I'll be right here at seven-t'irty. Pliz come."

But we wouldn't commit ourselves. However, we talked about the possibility all the way back to our pension. After all, it seemed such a harmless way to spend the evening. The atmosphere of the little café had been so pleasant, the proprietor and his family so friendly, there seemed no valid reason to hesitate.

As Rusty put it, "After all, it isn't exactly like going out with a man we picked up. The gondolier will just be there, too, that's all. And he was cute, don't you think?"

I had to agree that he was cute and also that the evening sounded completely unobjectionable. By the time we reached our pension, we had persuaded ourselves we'd be foolish not to spend Christmas Eve in as enjoyable a manner as possible.

We had plenty of time to shower and rest before getting dressed again. Flopped across the bed in our slips, we read our Christmas letters from home. Savoring each written word, sharing vicariously in all the pre-holiday activities the various members of the clan had told me about, it was almost like talking to them all, so much of themselves had gone into their letters. I felt choked up with emotion by the time I finished. And one look at Rusty indicated she was feeling the same way.

"We'd better get out and do something that's fun, or we'll be crying on each other's shoulders!" I exclaimed as I hopped off the bed and began getting dressed.

"Right!" Rusty echoed. "Let's be real festive, shall we?"

So we put on the dressiest clothes we had with us,

our highest heels, our sparkliest earrings. The street in front of our pension was bright and dry in the moonlight, belying its sorry condition of the early morning. When we boarded the commuter boat it was practically empty. But a few stops farther along we were amazed to see two American soldiers get on. The sight of those familiar uniforms in such an unlikely place really jolted us.

"Do you see what I see?" Rusty murmured incredulously.

I nodded. "Unless we're having halucinations."

The soldiers were quite young, our age or even less I'd guess, not bad-looking, but not really spectacular. One had red hair and freckles, the other was a rangy blond. And they both looked quite glum, the effect, I decided, of being alone in a strange land on Christmas Eve.

After our first glance at them, neither Rusty or I let our eyes stray in their direction. This wasn't easy, especially since we could feel their eyes practically boring holes in our heads. We went on with the casual talk we had been engaged in when they boarded the boat. But we weren't exactly surprised when, before long, the redhead cleared his throat and said timidly, "Ma'am—pardon me, but—but you're speaking *English*."

And his friend added in an equally hushed, unbelieving tone, "You—couldn't possibly be—Americans, could you?"

Some people might have been able to snub an inoffensive pair of young fellow countrymen under such circumstances, but not Rusty and I. In fact, we couldn't help bursting out laughing as we admitted that our nationality was the same as theirs.

"Well, glory be!" exclaimed the blond, with a wide grin.

And the freckled one said wonderingly, "Who said there wasn't any Santa Claus?"

By the time we reached our stop we had learned that Red was from Michigan and Terry from Utah, that they were taking advantage of their Christmas leave to see some of Italy and Switzerland and that the prospect of spending Christmas Eve so far from home and family had begun to get them down. They had no specific plans, but were simply heading for the center of town in the hope that something entertaining might be going on there. When they heard our intentions, they asked so hopefully if they couldn't join us at the friendly little café for dinner that we couldn't bear to say no.

And so it was that when we walked along the street in front of the Doges' Palace, there weren't just the two of us. We had become a gay and laughing foursome.

The sight of our gondolier friend, waiting expectantly at the exact spot he had designated earlier startled us slightly. Because he wasn't alone, either. He was accompanied by another black-haired, dark-eyed man of around his own age. Apparently the thought that this addition to our party might not meet with our approval hadn't occurred to him at all. But when he saw us arriving, already in the company of two young men, his brows drew together in a forbidding frown. And he and his friend exchanged a few confidential remarks in staccato Italian.

Then he asked us accusingly, waving toward the two soldiers, " 'Ow come?"

Rusty and I tried to explain that we hadn't figured

on a double date with him and some unknown person, that we had simply meant to eat at the little café, where he could have joined us if he cared to. These two American soldiers wanted to eat there, too. It was as uncomplicated as that.

But this didn't satisfy the gondolier. We gave up trying to make plain to him that, if we hadn't met Red and Terry, and had arrived all alone, we still wouldn't have accompanied two strange Italians along Venice's dark and narrow streets. When he continued to eye the two boys belligerently and try to persuade us to leave them and go with him and his friend, we just shook our heads firmly, said good-bye and walked off in the opposite direction, all thoughts of eating in the little restaurant dissipated by his unreasonable attitude.

"So that's that," I said regretfully. "I suppose it serves us right, but somehow he didn't seem at all like that this afternoon."

"Let's still have dinner together, though," Red said anxiously, "even if we don't go to that particular place."

"There's a supper club in that big hotel just off St. Mark's Square," Terry backed him up. "We can dance there."

Rusty and I both loved to dance.

The night club was small and swank, with a marvelous band. The food wasn't bad, either. All in all, we had a wonderful time, eating, dancing and sharing happy Christmas memories of homes and families. The hours slipped away and we four, strangers in a strange land, built up a warm wall of friendliness about us, through which the winds of loneliness couldn't penetrate.

Red and Terry wanted to take us home in a gondola,

as a climax for the occasion. But we decided against that. They'd been so nice all evening, there was no use pushing our luck too far. We said goodnight on the commuter boat where we had met, knowing that it was actually good-bye, that we'd never see each other again, but not caring really. Still, it did seem that some sort of kindly fate had brought us together, at that particular time and place, so that we could have a happier Christmas Eve and one that none of us was ever likely to forget.

13

SMALL ROMANCE IN FLORENCE

On Christmas morning we left for Florence. The sun shone brightly as we boarded our train, just as it had when we arrived. In between, it hadn't appeared at all.

Watching Venice slip away behind us, I said, "Maybe we didn't have a regulation tourist's view of the place, but we certainly got into the spirit of things while we were there."

Rusty nodded. "We met such interesting people, too."

The train ride was quite spectacular when we weren't going through pitch-dark tunnels. There were mountains all about and picturesque villages perched on the slopes and clustered in the valleys. We bought our lunch through the window from a platform vendor—apples and Cokes and a delicious Italian Christmas cake called *Motta*, rich with raisins.

It was quite warm when we reached Florence early in the afternoon and didn't feel a bit like Christmas, as we were accustomed to it in Iowa and Illinois. We had two possibilities as to places to stay. Some girls at the

Institute had suggested one hotel, our French professor had highly recommended another, where he had stayed several years ago. We inquired around the station, but no one had ever heard of the first place. However, Professor Wencelius had given us the approximate address of the one he liked. So we decided to try to find it.

We set out on foot, having discovered that no buses were running because of the holiday. Carrying anything heavy always bothers Rusty, so I took charge of our suitcase. Within a few blocks my arm began to get pretty tired and so, since the bag was cloth, I decided to try carrying it on my head, as peasant women carry their loads. And immediately I found out why they use this method; it's so much more comfortable than any other way.

"You look rather odd," Rusty said dubiously.

"So what? There's hardly anyone around to see."

This was quite true. The downtown streets were almost deserted. Everyone was apparently at home celebrating Christmas. Presently, though, a little man rushed up breathlessly from behind us. He had blond hair and a florid complexion and appeared to be around forty. In broken English, with a definite Italian accent, he asked if he could carry our bag.

Now we had been warned again and again about Italian men. We knew from experience their habit of looking girls over coolly from head to toe, with several rather embarrassing detours in between. Often they tried to start conversations right on the street and you simply had to ignore them. But this little man didn't seem remotely like a wolf and sometimes it's safe to trust your instincts in such matters. I murmured,

"Grazie," and let him take the suitcase.

He walked with us for blocks and blocks, looking for the professor's hotel. He spoke some French, but very little English; still we managed to carry on a conversation. We learned that his parents were dead, that he had no close family. He seemed dreadfully lonesome and reminded me of a dog who doesn't belong to anyone, but who tries hard to make friends and is grateful for the slightest attention, even a passing smile.

When we reached the street where the hotel was supposed to be, he made inquiries for us from several passers-by, but no one knew of it. Then our little man looked in the telephone directory, but was unable to find the name. So we decided the place must have closed in the years since the professor had stayed there.

"Now what?" I asked Rusty, but she didn't have any very constructive ideas, either.

Not so our new-found friend. His face alight with helpfulness, he offered to phone his landlady and ask if she knew of any nice pensions in the neighborhood where we were. This seemed a good suggestion, so we let him go ahead. The result was that he cheerfully lugged our suitcase another half mile to a place she recommended. We thanked him profusely, knowing he'd have been hurt had we offered him a tip. When we wished him a merry Christmas in farewell, the delighted look he gave us implied we'd done him a favor, instead of the other way around.

The pension was a very nice one and we were able to rent a clean, pleasant, though unheated room, with meals, for slightly under two dollars a day. And what meals! The first night we had homemade noodle soup, meat and vegetables, fruit and whipped-cream cake, all perfectly delicious. Moreover, the place was run by a friendly, exuberant family consisting of Mamma and Papa and several children. They were so aghast at the thought of two young girls all alone at Christmas time in a strange land that they took us right to their hearts and insisted on our sharing their holiday celebration. The crowd of relatives and friends that gathered in their ornately decorated parlor accepted us with great warmth and made us feel quite at home.

Among the guests were two students near our own age, Pietro and Tony. Tony lived at the pension and Pietro was his best friend. Tony was dark, of medium height; Pietro was taller and blond, with a nice shy smile and blue eyes that reminded me, rather absurdly, of those of my four-year-old nephew.

Now Rusty and I had an unwritten understanding in such situations; being shorter than I, she always took the shorter young man. This left Pietro for me. He was majoring in political science, I learned, but was interested in journalism and philosophy as well. With so many interests in common, plus a mutual knowledge of French, we didn't have a bit of trouble conversing. Rusty didn't fare as well with Tony, although he seemed attentive and pleasant enough. But he could speak only Italian and a little English, which made communication difficult for them.

When someone turned on the record player and we began to dance, Rusty and Tony got along much better. Pietro and I enjoyed it thoroughly, too. Soon the boys suggested going to a dance club in the neighborhood and Rusty and I agreed. Pietro and I rode his Vespa, which was parked outside. I'd been on a motor scooter only a few times before, although they're a common mode of transportation in Europe. Riding through the night was a wonderful sensation, almost like flying.

We waited outside the dance club for Rusty and Tony, who soon arrived on foot. There proved to be an excellent band and the crowd was young and gay, but not at all rowdy. When it was time to go, Rusty and I stopped in the powder room to compare notes.

"Do you mind walking back alone with Tony?" I asked.

"Not a bit," she smiled. "Go on and have fun."

As we settled ourselves on the scooter, Pietro turned to me. "How would you like to see the city from Michelangelo's Hill?"

"Is it far?" I queried, tempted.

He shook his head. "Only a few miles. We'll get back to the pension almost by the time the others can walk there."

"All right," I agreed. "It sounds beautiful."

We flew through the starry night, along narrow streets, then up and up in a slow steady ascent. The view from the top of the hill was breathtaking. Far below, all Florence was spread at our feet, her lights twinkling like a carpet of spilled jewels.

"No visitor should miss seeing this," Pietro said in his earnest young voice. "Don't you agree?"

"Oh, yes," I answered. "I've never seen anything lovelier."

I don't know how long we stood there, drinking in beauty, discussing the artists who had lived in Florence centuries ago and whose deathless works still graced her art galleries and museums. I hoped very hard that Pietro wouldn't spoil things by trying to take advantage of the fact that we had the place and the moment so completely to ourselves. After all, he was Italian, even if he didn't look it. And perhaps, in coming here with him, I had given him some encouragement, some grounds for misunderstanding.

But he didn't so much as touch me, which made me like him even better than before. In fact, it was he who said presently that we should be getting back, or Rusty might worry. All the way to the pension, I sat there with my arms wrapped around him—which is the way you have to ride a Vespa if you don't want to fall off!—and thought what a sweet guy he was and how lucky I'd been to meet him.

When Rusty and I were getting ready for bed, I asked if she'd had any trouble with Tony.

"No trouble," she yawned, "but he's not very exciting." I felt rather selfish, remembering the wonderful time I'd had with Pietro. Would I ever see him again, I wondered? At the moment, the answer to that question seemed quite important . . .

Rusty and I explored Florence the following day. The fourteenth-century Franciscan church of Santa Croce was an awe-inspiring sight, containing, as it did, the tomb of Michelangelo. We visited the Pitti Palace, with its lovely formal gardens and fabulous art display, and stood entranced before paintings by Botticelli, Raphael and countless other Italian masters. The city is built along both sides of the River Arno and there are several picturesque old bridges, some of which have shops right on them. Beautiful cathedrals and palaces tower on almost every street. We despaired of having time to see them all.

In the evening Pietro and Tony sought us out. Rusty begged off, with the excuse that she had to wash her hair and write some letters. I can't say I blamed her, in view of the language barrier between her and Tony. But Pietro and I had no such problem. We took off happily on his Vespa and rode through the blue Italian dusk to the top of "our" hill overlooking the city. Tonight we had more time, so we went for a long walk through the park and stopped at a little sidewalk café for chocolate. Then we rode back down into the city and stopped at another café, where we sat talking for hours. He told me about his school, the campus newspaper of which he was editor, and his philosophy of life. We discussed marriage, different European attitudes of thought, America's trend toward materialism and practically everything else under the sun. I hadn't had such a good solid conversation with an attractive man since Brad's and my fascinating talks last summer. No wonder I listened attentively to every word Pietro spoke, and then answered in such a way as to draw him out even further.

Both of us hated to see the evening end. We lingered in the street outside the pension, not saying too much, but understanding some things without words.

"It is rather sad, you and I," Pietro said gravely. "We meet, we enjoy being together, but for so short a while. If there were more time, we could be good friends. Of this I feel sure."

I nodded in agreement, my throat aching. "But—even if we haven't much time, I'm glad we met."

"I am glad, too." Pietro smiled and I could see the

white flash of his teeth under the streetlight. "I am glad because now, when I hear people say impatiently, 'Americans are thus and so. They do this and that. They are so different from us,' I will know they are wrong. Or, at least, that they are wrong about some Americans. I will know there are people in the United States who have respect for knowledge, who want to learn, just as we do, who strive to understand other people and their problems, their different way of life. I will know there are students there, just as here, who work hard to pay for their own education, like this Brad you tell me of, and so many others."

"And I'll understand Italians better, because of having met you," I told him.

"This is good," Pietro nodded, "this understanding, this closeness and sympathy. We must never forget."

"We won't," I agreed.

He pressed my hand briefly, smiling down into my face. We said good-bye and I went inside and shut the door after me. I felt like crying, but I wouldn't give in. What was there to cry about, for pity's sake, I asked myself fiercely as I went upstairs?

Rusty was asleep, so I undressed quietly in the dark and got into bed. I tried to fall asleep quickly, reminding myself that we had quite a sight-seeing schedule planned for the next day. The Uffizi Gallery, the Palazzo Vecchio, the Baptistry with its great bronze doors, so many places we hadn't had time for today. Then on to Rome in the late afternoon, where we planned to meet Dave Schultz.

Firmly I kept my thoughts pointed toward the future, concentrating on all the fun and excitement that still lay ahead. But this wasn't easy, with Pietro's shy smile drifting between me and the pleasures I was trying so hard to look forward to.

Lying there, wide-eyed in the darkness, I seemed to hear his voice again, saying so solemnly, "We must never forget."

As if I could, I thought bleakly. And I had a hunch he might have a little trouble, too, until enough time had elapsed to blur the sharp, hurting edges of memory.

14

NEW YEAR'S IN ROME

Rome was as fascinating, as ancient, as colorful and cosmopolitan as we had imagined it. We found a pleasant pension, recommended in advance by an Institute friend, where, by thrifty bargaining, we got a room with meals for three dollars a day apiece. Considering that Rome is one of the world's largest cities, this was quite an accomplishment. And the food! Great steaming plates of spaghetti were served as appetizers, with the main course to follow!

"If we get out of here without gaining ten pounds, we'll be lucky," Rusty said, enjoying every mouthful.

"Oh, well," I shrugged, "we can always diet at school."

We lost no time in picking up our mail at American Express. A lovely long letter from Brad helped push Pietro temporarily out of my thoughts. There was also a telegram from Dave, saying he'd arrive in Rome at six o'clock New Year's Eve.

"In a way," I confided to Rusty, "I'm just as glad we didn't travel with him all the time we were in Italy. I like Dave, but I doubt we'd have had nearly as exciting adventures."

"Or met such fascinating people," Rusty said drily.

We didn't accomplish much our first day in Rome, except to do a lot of window-looking in the perfectly fabulous shops and buy some beautiful Italian shoes. And Rusty phoned Steve. Quite suddenly around lunch-time she said she simply couldn't bear it a minute longer without talking to him. So she put through a long-distance call to Germany, which meant we had to hang around most of the afternoon waiting for the connection to be completed. It was worth it, though, as far as Rusty was concerned. And I felt good, too, just seeing how happy her brief talk with Steve left her.

The next morning we walked out of our room to go down to breakfast and there in the hall ran into four other kids from the Institute. Some of them had been to Austria, some to Switzerland, and here we were, without pre-arrangement, all stopping at the same pension. Naturally we had quite a reunion and made plans to celebrate New Year's Eve together the following day. Then Rusty and I went on over to American Express, where we signed up for four bus tours of the city, two for that day, two for the next. Up until now we had scorned such regimented methods of sight-seeing. But Rome is so large and there is so much to see, we felt we'd miss a lot if we tried doing it on our own.

The first day we saw so much we could scarcely absorb it all. The Pantheon, the ruins of the Forum, Capitoline Hill, the Trevi Fountain, St. Peter's. Each relic of an ancient civilization was fascinating in its own way. And we were tremendously impressed with the ornate golden inlays and mosaics, the world-famous paintings and sculpture that graced St. Peter's. At lunchtime we found, of all things, an American restaurant not far from the Express office. Here we had a blissfully nostalgic lunch, waffles, milk, hamburgers and chocolate sundaes, to sustain us through our afternoon sight-seeing. By evening we were far too tired, too glutted with all the rare and lovely things we had seen, to do more than write a few letters and get to bed early.

The next day was the last of the year. We spent most of the morning at the Vatican Museum, a treasure house of paintings and statues, and in the Sistine Chapel, where the ceiling frescoes were painted by Michelangelo. Then, since it happened to be the day on which the pope gave audience to tourists, we, along with hundreds of others, saw the pope. He was carried through the throng on a sort of throne, in rich robes and surrounded by colorfully dressed guards. It was an impressive spectacle of almost medieval splendor and Rusty and I were glad we hadn't missed it, even though we weren't Catholic.

After lunch—this time we had hamburgers, sodas and apple pie—we discovered upon reaching the starting point of our final bus tour that we were the only ones signed up for that trip. However, noting our disappointment, the guide had a small conference in Italian with the driver, and then informed us in his quaintly accented English that they wouldn't cancel the tour after all, provided we cared to take it. Naturally we did. The driver and guide were both fortyish and we felt sure riding around in a sixty-seat bus with them in broad daylight was quite safe.

We rode out along the Appian Way, then walked through the dark, creepy Catacombs, where the early Christians hid underground when they were persecuted for their beliefs. We saw several beautiful churches and some of the ancient gates that have stood ever since Rome was a walled city. The guide was most accommodating. He just asked where we wanted to go and what we wanted to see and then had the driver take us there. We even got to see some of the lovely countryside surrounding the city. And the driver went miles out of his way to drop us off near our pension. Talk about service!

We barely had time for a shower and a change of clothes before meeting Dave's train. It was fun to see him again and to hear about all he'd been doing. He was pleased to learn we were having a party that night, with the other Institute kids.

"We'll welcome the new year in style," he grinned.

And we certainly did. The seven of us sort of took over the lounge at the pension. We had bread, cheese, cold cuts, *Motta* cake and a mild white wine which even I enjoyed. We talked and laughed and played guessing games and grew quite hilarious as the end of the old year drew near. At midnight, we all rushed out into the street, since we had heard about some unique New Year's Eve customs of the Romans, which we didn't want to miss.

We hadn't been misinformed, either. At midnight they throw out all the old things they can find. Bottles, shoes, pots and pans, garbage, almost anything you can think of came crashing down into the street. We hugged the front of the building, so that none of the debris would land on us. I've never seen such a mess as the streets of Rome became in short order.

"When in Rome," Rusty stooped to pick up a bottle

which, miraculously, hadn't broken when it fell, "do as the Romans do!"

She tossed the bottle into the air and it splintered with a resounding crash on the pavement. After that, we all ran around breaking things, or simply tossing them into the air and letting them fall again, to hear the clatter. Presently, we went back inside and sat discussing everything under the sun until we were all too sleepy to stay awake any longer.

As we got into bed, I told Rusty, "It's not exactly like any other New Year's I've ever spent. But it was fun."

"Ummm," Rusty agreed. "And it's one we'll remember, too."

The three of us left Rome for Naples the following morning. We happened to share a compartment on the train with another American. When he heard us speaking English his face lit and he joined in the conversation without a moment's hesitation. His name was John Ames and he was a Ph.D. in physics, doing further research in Copenhagen. By the time we left the train we felt like old friends and were planning to join forces for our sight-seeing.

As Rusty put it when we were alone, "He's not exactly terrific, but he seems nice. And a foursome's more fun than a threesome, so I'm glad we bumped into him."

We found a pension without any trouble and spent the rest of the day walking through the narrow streets of the city. Naples is a beautiful place, built on hills, as is San Francisco. The weather was wonderfully warm and sunny, the sky a bright clear blue. There was only one flaw. In so many parts of the city we saw evidence of appalling poverty. Houses were run-down and an atmosphere of squalor prevailed. True, it was picturesque squalor, but this probably didn't make it any easier to live in. Soon we had given away all our change to the ragged, bare-foot children who seemed to pop up on every side.

We escaped them in a beautiful park near the bay, from which we could see the blue Mediterranean and, in the distance, Capri and Vesuvius. But even when the little waifs no longer surrounded us, I couldn't seem to get them out of my mind. The thought of children, some of them no older than my little nieces and nephews, hungry and begging in the streets, would have seemed incredible to me back in America. Now I had seen it for myself and the memory would haunt me for a long time.

The next morning the four of us ascended Mt. Vesuvius. We went by bus to within a thousand feet or so of the top, then by chair-lift the rest of the way. This was much like a ski-lift, except that two people sat together and we were never much more than twenty feet from solid ground. From the top, the view of Naples and the bay far below, the vista of other mountains and valleys, was awesome.

Then, with a guide, we proceeded to walk around and part way down into the ancient crater itself. Some of the rocks were too hot to touch and the steam which rose all the time kept fogging John's and Dave's glasses. The eeriness of the place reminded me of pictures I once saw of Dante's Inferno.

We ate lunch in the extremely poor little town at the foot of the mountain, then went on to Pompeii. This was truly fascinating. The entire city was buried in A.D. 79 when Mt. Vesuvius erupted. Most of it has now been excavated, and to walk around among these ancient buildings was like stepping backward in time.

All of us got a great kick out of exploring and discussing everything, clambering around over grassy mounds, into every open gate we saw and over some that weren't open. The result was we lost all track of time and stayed so late that the exit gate was locked by the time we reached it. And the attendant had gone.

"Now what?" Rusty asked a shade apprehensively.

"We can't spend the night here," I said. "Vesuvius might erupt again." But in spite of my light tone, I, too, felt a slightly sinking sensation in my tummy.

"We'll have to climb over, that's all," Dave said. "Come on, John, we'll give them a boost."

Luckily it wasn't a very high gate. The only casualties were a run in my stocking and a broken fingernail for Rusty. It could have been much worse, we all agreed.

"Just think," Rusty said wistfully that night as we got ready for bed, "tomorrow will be our last day in Italy."

"It's really lived up to expectations, hasn't it?" I murmured. "And tomorrow Capri! That ought to afford a fitting climax for the whole trip."

"Oh, yes," Rusty agreed. "It sounds so romantic!"

The weather was cloudy the next morning, but we caught the island boat at nine-thirty. Scarcely were we out of the harbor when the gale struck. Or maybe it was a typhoon. I'm not really up on my sea storms. All I knew was that I'd never seen such rough water, not even crossing the Atlantic. The boat was only about seventy-five feet long. but it seemed seaworthy enough.

This didn't keep it from rocking wildly, though, with a sort of bucking-bronco motion. I'm sure it was a much rougher crossing than usual, because the ship's dishes, stored in special cabinets as they were, kept falling out and breaking all over the floor.

The majority of the passengers became violently seasick, or, as the French say, they suffered *mal de mer*. This sounds more glamorous, but the results are the same. We four were lucky. By staying outside and nibbling soda crackers and keeping our minds on other things, we survived the hour's trip in pretty good shape.

Capri is a perfect little gem of an island. It reminded me of Mackinac, with its horses and buggies, the small, clean towns and beautiful scenery. It's only a few miles long and has high rocky hills with roads cut around them. We walked up one of these roads and saw a perfectly gorgeous view from the top. En route we passed an ancient villa, built into the side of the hill as though it had grown there.

All day long the skies remained gray and overcast, so we decided to skip the motor boat trip to the Blue Grotto. There were enough other fascinating things to see. Just before we left the island, it began to rain in earnest. And our reverse crossing was even rougher than the first had been. But again we were lucky and remained unaffected by the boat's mad rolling and tossing.

Back in Naples there was only time for us to pack our bag, have a final dinner with Dave and catch our train. Dave saw us off and as we waved good-bye to him from our compartment window, I felt a warm glow of thankfulness for our friendship, firmly re-established now by all the time we had spent together the past few days.

We might never meet again, I realized. Still our long talks, the crazy things we'd done, would make our European experience richer for each of us than if we'd never met at all.

"I'm dead," Rusty sighed. "Do you suppose we'll be lucky enough to get some sleep on our way back to France?"

"Let's stretch out and try it, anyway," I said, yawning.

The night passed uneventfully. We didn't have the compartment all to ourselves, still we weren't too crowded. We slept fitfully through the train's starts and stops, its switchings and joltings. We had become quite adept at sleeping while we traveled. Neither of us, unfortunately, was remotely aware that we had made a horrible mistake in boarding this particular section of the train to Marseilles. Sometime during the night our car was uncoupled and transferred to a train heading, not toward Ventimiglia, where we expected to cross the border, but for Torino, much farther north in Italy. While we slept like babies we were being carried on and on, toward a destination well over a hundred miles from where we thought we were going!

15

DISASTER

No inkling of our big booboo marred our awakening that sunny Sunday morning. True, the landscape beyond the train's windows looked a bit more mountainous than we remembered. But, after all, we were approaching Ventimiglia, or so we innocently supposed, from a different direction than before, which could account for this impression. We decided the train must be running considerably behind schedule, or we'd have reached the border before this. Still, trains can be late in any country, so this didn't worry us, either.

When we finally pulled into a station where everyone began getting off, we gathered our things together hastily and joined the descending throng. This had to be the border, the end of the line, we felt sure. We'd been in so many Italian railway stations by that time, they all looked alike to us. And since no one around spoke English or French, we couldn't ask questions.

We stood hesitant for a moment, there on the platform, trying to get our bearings. "Do you remember where we went through customs?" I asked Rusty.

She shook her head. "I haven't the vaguest idea."

I picked up our suitcase, leaving Rusty with only her

umbrella to carry and a box containing a beautiful sweater she had bought for Steve in Rome. We trudged about, looking for the customs desk, but we couldn't find it. Our inquiries elicited nothing but shrugs and the helpless spreading of hands at which the Italians are so adept.

"You know what," I said finally, a great light breaking over me. "I'll bet we go through customs on the French side of the border! We were checked through here on our way into Italy. It must work the same way in reverse."

"Sounds logical," Rusty agreed. "So?"

"So let's stop worrying about customs and ask when we can get a train for Marseilles," I suggested.

And that was exactly what we did. This brought forth the dampening information that we faced a three-hour wait and would have to change trains at Savona. Neither of us had the foggiest notion where Savona was, nor did we especially care. It was the prospect of that three-hours' delay that we found maddening. Now there was no chance of our reaching Aix by mid-afternoon, as we had hoped to.

"Oh, well," I tried to be philosophical about it. "We'll have plenty of time for breakfast."

"And then we can write some letters," Rusty added.

Having eaten, we settled down to our correspondence in the station waiting room. And so intent did we become on describing our recent fascinating travels for our families' benefit, that neither of us paid much attention to the nondescript man with a trench coat over his arm who sat down next to Rusty on the long wooden bench. In Italy a man will always choose to sit needlessly close to a pretty girl, even though there's plenty of empty space around. Rusty just edged a little nearer to me and ignored him, so he soon rose and departed.

We went on writing. Not until Rusty had finished her letter and begun looking for a stamp, did she make a horrifying discovery. "Judy!" the note of panic in her voice yanked me out of my own concentration. "My passport case—it's gone!"

"Oh, Rusty, it can't be," I said soothingly, knowing her propensity for mislaying things. "Did you look in—"

"It is!" Rusty insisted. She frowned, trying to remember. "When we opened the suitcase to get our stationery—I had it then. I—I guess I took it out of my purse when I was looking for my pen. And then it was right here by me—" she broke off, her brown eyes wide and filled with anguish. "That man! He must have taken it!"

"What did he look like?" Panic mounted in me, too, as we both scrabbled around frantically through our pockets and purses and on the floor beneath us, but found no sign of the missing case.

"I don't know," Rusty said in a small voice. "He had a trench coat, that's all I remember. I hardly looked at him."

We peered anxiously about the waiting room. Half the men in it had trench coats. Besides, a thief wouldn't be likely to linger at the scene of the crime after he'd made his haul. By this time there wasn't a chance of finding him.

Rusty went on desperately, "It's not only my passport—all my ID cards—my traveler's checks—" Her voice broke.

"And your Italian train ticket," I recalled.

"And both our tickets from the border to Marseilles. I put them in the case for safekeeping, remember? Judy —" Rusty's voice was a wail of dismay, "what are we going to do?"

"Well, for one thing," I glanced ruefully at my watch and tried to sound more calm than I really felt, "we're going to miss our train. So that leaves us plenty of time to—to do whatever we have to do. Come on, we'll ask the ticket agent."

It wasn't easy to make our predicament clear to the man behind the barred window, but he finally got the gist of what we were trying to tell him. His big black eyes grew wide with sympathetic horror at the thought of such a monumental disaster. And he directed us to the nearest police station to report it.

Luckily the officer in charge understood a little English. He listened to our account of what had happened and pointed out the unlikelihood of ever catching the thief, since neither of us could possibly identify him. An American passport, he admitted with a regretful wag of his head, could bring a great deal of money on the black market. He proceeded to ask us countless questions and fill out an interminable form.

When he had finished, I asked, "Can you give us some sort of paper explaining what happened, something to show at the border when we leave Italy?"

His thick brows drew together in a forbidding frown. "But she—" he pointed at Rusty, "cannot leave till she gets another passport."

My heart sank. More explanations, I thought, more forms and red tape, more delay.

"But where do I get one?" Rusty gulped.

"The United States consulate," the officer said. Then he shook his head sadly. "Too bad it is closed on Sunday."

"You mean—I'll have to wait till tomorrow?" Rusty sounded sunk.

And I asked, "Couldn't we reach some official today in an emergency like this?"

"Quite impossible," the officer accented the third syllable of the word. "You must wait till morning."

Dejectedly we made our way out to the street and back to the railway station once more. It was almost two o'clock, well past lunchtime, but neither of us felt like eating. We huddled in the familiar waiting room for a conference. The more we talked it over, the larger our problem loomed. We were due back at the Institute in time for classes Monday morning. If neither of us showed up, there would be considerable anxiety as to our whereabouts. Mr. Maza might be sufficiently concerned to contact the police, or even our parents by cable. All sorts of complications could ensue, which we shuddered to think of.

We considered phoning Aix, but calls from one country to another are no simple matter. It had taken Rusty hours to call Steve. Besides, there was the matter of money. Our remaining funds were rather skimpy, considering that they'd have to stretch to cover train fares, a hotel for the night, several additional meals, plus who knew what charge for a new passport. Unquestionably, we were in a mess!

"Judy," Rusty said, "there's just one way to handle this. You take the first train you can get and explain everything to them at school. I'll stay here overnight and straighten things out at the consulate tomorrow morning. I'll only be a day late and, so long as they know why, there'll be no problem."

It did sound logical, put that way. Still I felt like a rat deserting a sinking ship at the idea of leaving her all alone. "Are you absolutely sure you can manage?" I asked dubiously.

"Of course," Rusty's voice was firm. "I'll go to a hotel right near the station. You see how soon you can get a train."

It developed that a train left for Savona in just fifteen minutes, which meant we had to reach a quick decision. The upshot was that I took it. But first we divided our remaining money. I kept just enough to cover my expenses back to Aix, leaving Rusty what we both felt was ample for a hotel room, her meals and transportation, plus a little left over to cover any charges attendant on getting another passport.

"You take the suitcase," Rusty said. "Then I won't have to bother with it."

She looked so pretty and helpless, standing there on the platform with her umbrella in one hand and Steve's sweater box clutched to her heart, that dismay mounted in me. "You're quite sure—" I began. But just then the conductor called the Italian equivalent of, "Alllll Abbbbaaarrrdd," and I had to rush off. Her, "I'll be all right," sounded not too reassuringly in my ears.

I settled down unhappily in a compartment. Had I done the right thing? On the other hand, what else could I do? It was all so complicated, there were so many angles to consider. And, after all, Rusty was no child. What could possibly happen to her? Gradually, my fears and uncertainties lessened. Then the conductor came through the train and I handed him my Italian ticket, which, luckily, I'd been carrying myself and so hadn't lost.

When I found he could speak French, I asked him how long it would take to reach Savona.

"About four hours," was his polite answer.

"Four *hours?*" I repeated incredulously. "But how can that be? Aren't we just a couple of stops from the border?"

"Oh, no, Mademoiselle," he shook his head. "Come, I'll show you." There was a big map at the end of the aisle and on it he patiently pointed out to me just where we were, where Savona was, where the border angled between Italy and France. Gradually, with the friendly old conductor's help, I finally realized how we must have taken the wrong car last night and so ended up far from our supposed destination, more than a hundred miles that now had to be retraced before reaching Ventimiglia on the border. Poor Rusty, the thought stabbed through me. She was going to find out she was a lot farther from Aix than she supposed, just as I was learning it now. But there was nothing I could do to soften the blow for her. The train wheels clicking away so rhythmically reminded me of that.

I had quite a trip! What with changing trains at Savona, I ended up in Nice at one-thirty in the morning. Not knowing where to look for a hotel at that hour, I spent the rest of the night sleeping fitfully in the railway waiting room. My train to Marseilles was late, so I finally reached Aix at ten-thirty, completely beat and with a dull throb of worry over Rusty aching in my mind. Luckily my first class didn't meet until eleven o'clock, so I made it. But the whole of that day remained pretty much of a blank for me. I explained to Rusty's professors why she wasn't in class. And after several tries I succeeded in getting hold of Mr. Maza to let him know of her predicament.

But he had already had a phone call from Torino. He told me, "The consul there required some verification of her story. It's all straightened out now, though. Don't worry."

His reassuring smile helped drive the gnawing uneasiness from my mind. And I was glad I'd had this bit of good news before a scowling Steve cornered me in French class and demanded, "What's this I hear about Rusty having her passport stolen?"

The relief in his face when I repeated what Mr. Maza had told me was wonderful to see. "I'll feel much better when she gets here, though," he admitted. "Think of her having to cope with a mess like that—" his voice got all husky with feeling.

"I know," I soothed. "But it's all right now."

I was too tired to worry much myself. I moved numbly through the rest of that endless day. Rusty still hadn't returned when I crawled wearily into bed right after dinner. But she'll be here soon, I mumbled into my pillow.

And that was the last I remembered until sunshine streaming into the room awakened me the next morning. Naturally my first conscious thought sent my anxious glance toward Rusty's bed. To my utter consternation, it was still empty.

16

RUSTY'S PLIGHT

Luckily, Rusty appeared just as I finished dressing. I don't believe I could have borne much longer the wild doubts, the frantic imaginings, the unanswerable questions that throbbed in my mind. At the sound of the door opening, I whirled around and saw shuffling toward me the most forlorn, bedraggled, hollow-eyed, dirty-faced creature imaginable, still clutching her umbrella and Steve's sweater box to her bosom.

"Rusty!" I gasped, flying to give her a big hug. "What happened?" Even as I asked, I propelled her toward the nearest bed before she should collapse completely.

Passing the mirror, she caught a glimpse of herself and her indomitable grin flashed. "If my sorority sisters could see me now," she muttered, "they wouldn't believe it!"

"I don't believe it, either," I admitted, as we sat down side by side on the edge of her bed. "Tell me all!"

Well, it was a long story, which, in retrospect seemed funny, although it certainly wouldn't have struck anyone that way while she was living through it. Maybe it was relief on Rusty's part at being home again, on mine at having her safely back, that made us both grow almost hysterical as she recounted the fantastic details of her harrowing experience.

She had felt pretty sunk, she confided, as she watched my train pull out. Not that she blamed me for leaving. She insisted she'd have done the same thing in my place. Still. her situation was rather scary and she didn't want to think too much about it.

"I decided to buy my train ticket right away," Rusty explained. "But on my way to the ticket window I passed a book stand and there—in English, imagine?—was a copy of Huxley's *Brave New World*, which I'd always wanted to read. So I bought it. After all, I had a lot of time to kill and I felt I had to have something to keep my mind off my troubles."

It was from the ticket agent that Rusty learned what I hadn't discovered until I was speeding along on the train—that we weren't in Ventimiglia and that the border was much farther away than we'd figured. To Rusty's horror, her ticket cost almost all the money she had. So there was no choice but to spend the night in the station waiting room. Moreover, she didn't even have enough money for a regular dinner. So, fortified with a couple of candy bars, she proceeded to alternately doze and read *Brave New World* through all those interminable hours until morning.

"Daylight never looked so good to me," she admitted. "I learned that the consulate didn't open till nine, so that left plenty of time to clean up a little. But you know European washrooms—they never supply soap. And I couldn't do much with cold water. I was getting pretty hungry, too, but I hated to spend the few lire I had left and be absolutely broke. I kept thinking, It'll be all right when I get to the consulate. They'll give me another passport and advance me some money. All I have to do is hang on till nine."

It was Rusty's account of what happened at the consulate that nearly broke both of us up completely. There she had stood in the cold light of morning, her clothes wrinkled, her face and hands none too clean, claiming to be an American student who had been traveling in Italy for the past two weeks and whose passport and traveler's checks had been stolen.

"Traveling with no luggage except an umbrella and a box containing a man's sweater?" I could just hear the consular official's skeptical tone as Rusty described the scene.

"I had to explain in minute detail," Rusty told me, "all about you taking our suitcase and why you had to go and exactly what had happened. And of course I didn't have a shred of identification. They seemed to think I was a very clever Italian who had made up the whole fantastic story just so I could get out of Italy for some reason, probably criminal. I've never answered so many questions in my life. And all the time I was getting hungrier and more tired. It was really a nightmare. I couldn't even think very clearly by that time, but at last it occurred to me to suggest they call the Institute and talk to Mr. Maza. And, of course, he verified my identity right away. But there were still yards of red tape to go through and all sorts of forms to fill out before I could get a temporary passport. Then, as a final climax, they said I'd have to have my picture taken."

Weary, grimy, weak with lack of food, Rusty sat for a

passport photo. It was a little gem, too, even more ghoulishly unflattering than such pictures usually are. Then, on the way down the stairs from the photographer's studio, the past hours suddenly caught up with her and she collapsed in a heap. "I have no idea how I got back to the consulate," Rusty admitted, "but I came to with the lovely aroma of hot soup in my nostrils. Nothing ever smelled so good!"

The food revived her considerably. And the consulate authorized an advance of enough money to see her back to Aix. Luckily, on the train, Rusty ran into a pleasant young English couple who had stayed at the same pension with us in Rome. They had with them a former Yale man, now a Fulbright student, who was quite attractive, according to Rusty. But even though her trip as far as Nice had been gay, she was too slap-happy to enjoy it.

"I thought I'd never get here," she confided with a long sigh. "Now that I've made it, I'm going to bed and sleep all day and all night and maybe all day tomorrow. Don't you dare wake me."

"I won't," I promised.

I helped her out of her dirty, wrinkled clothes and into bed, then drew the drapes and tiptoed away quietly. What a time the poor kid had had! If she never wanted to take another trip, I couldn't really blame her. But it would be a shame if her unhappy experience had that effect. After all, mid-semester break would be coming up in less than a month, as soon as exams were over. That meant two whole weeks free, a wonderful chance to go somewhere, Austria, perhaps, or Spain. We'd even discussed various possibilities earlier. Now, though—well, I'd just have to wait and see.

As a matter of fact, I didn't have to wait very long. Rusty woke up at six that night, completely rested, but starved. After dinner, she had a date with Steve. I spent part of the evening talking with Joan Thomas, the rest reading Sartre and Camus for European lit. I had just gone to bed when Rusty came in. There was a dreamy look in her brown eyes and her lipstick was pretty well kissed off. She came over and perched on the edge of my bed and just sat for a time, staring off mistily into space.

Then she said, "Judy, I think I'm in love."

"That's nice," I said. "Have a good reunion?"

She nodded. Then she asked with a faint frown, "How can you tell for sure whether you're in love or not?"

"If I had a set of absolutely dependable rules," I smiled, "I'd write a book on the subject and make a fortune."

Rusty went on, "I know I never felt this way about anyone before—so good, so—warm and happy when we're together. Is it like that when you're with Brad?"

"Yes," I said softly, "that's exactly how it is." My need for him swelled in me till I could scarcely stand the ache of it. Absurdly I felt tears press against my eyelids.

But Rusty didn't notice, so intent was she on her own feelings. She told me, "Seeing Steve tonight—well, honestly, it seemed we'd been apart for years instead of weeks. He felt that way, too. He said he was so worried, he was ready to start for Italy to look for me." A tender little smile played around her mouth.

"He sounded worried," I nodded, "when I talked to him yesterday. It's a good thing you got back when you did."

"And you know what?" Rusty brought her eyes back to my face. "He wants me to go to Innsbruck skiing between semesters. Several kids are dreaming up a trip there already. You'd go, too, wouldn't you?"

"Oh, I might." A feeling of relief poured through me. Actually, the thought of a ski trip didn't especially send me. I'd hardly been on skis in my life. But it delighted me that Rusty was looking forward so soon to some more travels, after her shattering experience. Where she went didn't matter so much, just the mere fact that she was willing to go somewhere. It was a little like falling off a horse, I reflected. The important thing was to get back into the saddle immediately.

Those next few weeks were filled with studying. Actually our mid-semester exams didn't prove as stiff as we had feared they might, and both Rusty and I acquitted ourselves creditably. It was also during this part of the year that we encountered the mistral, an indescribable wind which blows in the south of France and has no counterpart anywhere else on earth. No matter how mild the temperature, that eerie stabbing wind seems to come from nowhere and everywhere and can cut through you like a knife and leave your teeth chattering with its raw chill.

Gradually our vacation plans fell into place. After a good deal of thought, I decided not to go to Innsbruck with Rusty. The crowd that was planning to ski there broke down into pretty solid twosomes and I didn't feel I'd especially fit in. Instead, Joan Thomas and I planned to go to Switzerland and Vienna together. I liked Joan and thought she'd make a good travel companion. In fact, we were a good deal alike in personality, which made us quite congenial. As well as we got along, though, I was glad things hadn't worked out so that we roomed together all year. It had been a much more enriching experience to live with someone like Rusty, who wasn't at all like me. I wouldn't have missed that for the world.

Saying good-bye gave us both a real jolt. We had been together so constantly during our months in Europe that it seemed incredible to think of not seeing each other for almost two weeks.

"Hang onto that passport now," I admonished, having gone to the bus terminal to see Rusty and the others off.

"Don't worry!" she said grimly. "I learned my lesson."

And Steve, big and solid and protective beside her, added, "I'll see that she does."

"Remember now," Rusty told me in parting, "to look us up if you get to Innsbruck. We'll leave word at American Express."

"I will." I waved good-bye as the bus pulled out, then hurried back to the Pavillon to start packing for my own travels.

Compared to some of the train rides I'd had with Rusty, Joan's and my trip to Berne proved uneventful. We did get to talking with a young Italian, whose limited grasp of French led him to believe we were of that nationality. It was fun fooling him for a while. But when he learned we were really Americans, his interest increased immeasurably. Like so many of his countrymen, he wanted desperately to come to America and felt he only needed someone to "call him over," that is, sponsor him. We declined sympathetically and tactfully. But in spite of our assurances that everyone back home wasn't rich and that jobs were sometimes hard to come by, he still seemed convinced that one had only to step foot in the United States in order to acquire a large fortune and live like a king.

It was very cold in Berne and there wasn't really too much to see there, although we enjoyed the warm friendliness of the people. Joan and I stayed at a youth hostel, the first of these I'd tried. One hears and reads so much about European hostels, but they vary a great deal in different countries. For instance, in France they are not at all clean or appealing. A decent girl would hesitate to stay in one there. But our accommodations in Berne were wonderful and we were to find the same high standards prevailing all over Switzerland. It cost only forty cents apiece to stay overnight. We were expected to be in by ten p.m. and to sweep our room when we were ready to leave, but such minor regulations didn't bother us.

Both Joan and I loved bridge and our first night at the hostel we decided to do our darnedest to find a couple more players so that we could have a game. We pounced on each young person who entered the lounge, but with a notable lack of success. Finally, it struck us that a great many people seemed to be assembling. To our embarrassment, it developed that a meeting was about to take place, a serious discussion in German of local school problems. And here we two had been asking all the participants if they wouldn't like to play bridge! We withdrew as unobtrusively as possible and sneaked off to bed.

The next morning right after breakfast we took a train up into the mountains to Interlaken. We couldn't see much during the trip because of the heavy fog beyond the windows. And when we arrived, Interlaken itself seemed disappointingly flat and mist-shrouded, with a closed-up-for-the-winter air about it. We strolled around aimlessly, debating whether to go back to Berne and hope for better weather tomorrow. Then we decided, half against our better judgment, to take the electric railway still farther up into the mountains, to the village of Grindelwald, where we might be lucky enough to catch at least a glimpse of the famous peaks that surrounded the village.

And what a fabulous trip that was! As soon as we started up, we got out of the fog. All about us, stretching off into the distance, were snow-covered peaks, forests of evergreens, the delicate tracery of frozen waterfalls. Picturesque villages and isolated chalets nestled on the steep slopes and huddled in the valleys. Grindelwald itself was a fairytale setting, with darling shops, skiers in bright clothes everywhere and a skating pond on which young and old were skimming about joyously. The quaint wooden houses had ornately carved doors and balconies and were surrounded by prim little fences, their posts sticking up through the snow. And circling it all were the great mountain peaks, rugged against the bright blue sky.

It was mid-afternoon before we could tear ourselves away from such a feast of beauty. When we got back to Interlaken, an incredible change had take place there.

With the lifting of the fog that had closed it in earlier, we found that it, too, afforded an awe-inspiring view of mountains and lakes. Even the silvery peak of the Jungfrau was visible above the clouds.

We reached our hostel in Berne just at dinnertime. And both Joan and I were too tired, too drunk with the beauty we had reveled in all day, to do more than eat ravenously and crawl into bed, like the pair of tourists we were.

17

THE LOVELY LIPIZZANS

We spent two more days touring Switzerland. In Lucerne and Zurich we were impressed not only by the beauty of the scenery, but by the museums and cathedrals, too. The Swiss are very friendly and language was no problem at all. Everyone spoke English or French or German. And since Joan knew a bit of the latter, we could communicate freely. In every restaurant the food was delicious and the prices reasonable. We could even get good pure milk to drink, a treat for both of us. The shopping was also excellent and we splurged on lovely sweaters and hand-made blouses.

But much as we loved Switzerland, we were looking forward to Austria, too, so we headed that way on Thursday. We could have gone straight through to Vienna, our ultimate destination, but we wanted to stop in Innsbruck for two reasons. It would be fun to see Rusty and the other Institute kids; besides, neither of us wanted to miss all the spectacular Tyrolian scenery by traveling through it at night.

So we piled off our train at ten-thirty at the Innsbruck

station and stood there on the platform for a moment, trying to get our bearings.

I asked in a tentative sort of tone, "Do you think we should start looking around for a hotel?"

"It's so late," Joan replied promptly. "Can't we just sleep in the waiting room?"

I grinned. "I was hoping you'd feel that way. Let's."

It's funny how one's viewpoint changes. Back in America such an idea wouldn't have occurred to us. But in Europe many students save money this way. And we were both the adaptable type.

We stretched out in the first-class waiting room because it had comfortable padded benches. Of course, we were traveling second class, but they aren't very fussy about which waiting room you use. With our purses as pillows and our suitcases for arm-rests, we slept like babies till morning.

Stretching, Joan said, "I always like a firm mattress."

"Wonderful for the spine," I agreed.

We got cleaned up and had breakfast, then set out in search of our friends. But the message they had left informed us that they had gone on to Seefeld, farther up in the mountains. We shrugged off our disappointment and decided to spend the few hours we had before train time in sight-seeing. Actually, Innsbruck is quite an interesting place. The capital of the Tyrol, it is situated on both sides of the Inn River. We explored an ancient church and a couple of palaces. By that time our feet were tired, so we went back to the station and played two-handed bridge till our train left.

Speeding through the spectacular Austrian scenery, we were glad we had waited to enjoy it by daylight. Then, as we neared the end of our journey, Joan asked, "Do you know what I always think of in connection with Vienna?"

"Waltzes? Romance?"

She shook her head. "Horses. Did you ever hear of those Lipizzans that are so marvelously trained?"

I leaned forward enthusiastically. "Did I! Why, you're talking to an old horse-lover, girl. I've read all about Lipizzans. I even had pictures of them in my bedroom when I was little."

"You too?" Joan grinned.

A train of thought had been started which was difficult to stop. I went on reminiscently, "I read every horse book I could lay my hands on. I took riding lessons. When I was ten, I decided I'd never marry anyone but a rancher, or at least a cowboy. My long-suffering parents even got me a horse, which I had till I started college. I used to take full care of her, too—fed and watered her, cleaned her stall—the works!"

"Lucky!" Joan said. "I never owned a horse, but I did all the rest of it. We'd have got along nicely as children."

"But Lipizzans!" I exclaimed, feeling excitement mount in me. "I'd forgotten Vienna was where they are."

Joan nodded almost reverently. "Maybe we can see them."

Our first morning in Vienna, we took a bus tour of the usual parks, notable buildings and monuments, which was climaxed by a trip through the Imperial palace. This proved much less drafty, damp and dull than most palaces. The rooms were ornate, but beautifully decorated and had an almost lived-in air. Next we went to the opera, hoping to get tickets for Saturday night. But that performance was sold out, so we had to settle for Sunday. Vienna is a very cultural city and music is the most popular form of entertainment. In fact, we had noted an interesting fact earlier. There are more monuments to composers than warriors.

After lunch, we window-shopped our way to the Spanish Riding School, where the Lipizzan horses are trained and kept. Never had either of us spent a more fascinating afternoon. The Lipizzans are a special breed, pure white, powerfully built and unforgettably beautiful. The Spanish Riding School was started centuries ago by the royal family and maintained at first for their pleasure. Now it has become a national institution. There the Lipizzans are trained to do the most complex and graceful quadrilles and other difficult dance steps. They are the true ballet stars of the horse kingdom. And people come from all over the world to watch them go through their marvelous maneuvers.

Naturally a pair of horse enthusiasts like Joan and me were utterly enchanted. We practically went into orbit when we were permitted to walk around in the stables and actually pet those proud, yet friendly stallions. Finally we had to be politely requested to leave because it was feeding time. But we were told that, if we cared to, we could return Monday morning and watch some of the actual training process. *If* we cared to!

"You couldn't keep me away," Joan said, as we walked back toward our pension.

I nodded, adding, "I feel as though I had personally met a movie star—and one I got to rub noses with, too!"

We enjoyed every bit of our stay in Vienna. There was

an infinite variety of things to see and do. The opera we went to was "Salome" and while the prima donna was a bit hefty, especially when she did her dance of the seven veils, the singing was adequate. And the opera house itself was gorgeous, all white and gold and deep red velvet. The first floor crowd was very glamorous to look down on, the women in low-cut dresses and glittering jewels, the men in dinner jackets or even tails. Joan and I sat high up in the balcony with the rest of the students and were struck by the rapt attention and obvious appreciation in the faces all around us.

Sunday night we made a truly epic discovery—an American restaurant. So for dinner I had two hamburgers and a banana split. Such places are always tourist traps, of course. But the familiar food was well worth the price, both of us figured.

Early on Monday we rushed once more to the Spanish Riding School, where for several glorious hours we watched the training of the Lipizzans. Serious, ram-rod erect, classical riders took the lovely white horses through the intricate figures over and over, with infinite patience and firmness. The horses, though majestically proud, were at the same time eager to please. And the spirit of teamwork between animal and man was marvelous to observe.

Leaving, both Joan and I knew we had seen something we would never forget . . .

When we took a train from Austria, we were very careful to board the right car. After Rusty's and my harrowing time getting lost in Italy, I was taking no chances. It was a long trip, with several changes and stop-overs. Joan left the train in Venice, which she hadn't visited before.

I went on to Milan, where I intended to stop for at least a day. But suddenly, as the train pulled into that city and I began gathering my things together to get off, I was overwhelmed by the strangest sensation. I felt homesick! Only not for home, really—for Rusty and Aix and our familiar cozy room at the Pavillon. It was crazy!

Moved by an irresistible impulse, I shoved my suitcase back onto the luggage rack and settled once more into my seat. There wasn't a thing in Milan I was mad to see. So why not just go on my way and get into Aix a day early? I'd have more time to do all the little odd jobs I'd been allowing to accumulate. And I could relax a bit before the start of the new semester on Monday.

The rest of the trip passed uneventfully. A nice, quite attractive young Italian got on the train in Milan and sat down opposite me. Soon we were joined by a motherly-looking woman from Israel. The young man was eager to talk, but he spoke only Italian and German. Fortunately the lady from Israel knew German and French, so she obligingly interpreted for us. But this was a bit tricky and didn't help the free flow of ideas very much. Now and then the Italian would look at me regretfully, shake his head and say, "*Ah Mademoiselle, je ne peux pas parler*," which meant, "I can't speak," and was apparently all the French he knew.

He did prove quite helpful, though, when I had to change trains in Genoa. He carried my suitcase and saw me onto the right car of the right train for Nice. If only, I thought as we waved good-bye, countries could get along as amicably as can the people of those countries when chance throws them together, it would be a wonderful thing and the hope of peace would brighten.

Rusty and I had a fine reunion. She had got back a few hours ahead of me and was on hand to welcome me home. It was so great to be together again, we talked for hours and hours, telling each other all about our adventures apart. Rusty and the others had had a wonderful time in Austria, indulging in various winter sports for which the region is famous. But I wouldn't have missed for the world the things Joan and I had seen and done. So neither of us had any regrets, even though we'd missed each other.

I found a stack of mail awaiting me, including a couple of long letters from Brad. Naturally I read these first and when I had finished them, I sat for a while staring off into space with a slight frown. Maybe it was just because I was tired from my long train ride, or I might be imagining things, but there was something in Brad's letters that bothered me.

"Is anything wrong?" Rusty's sympathetic voice broke into my abstraction.

"No-o," I shook my head, but my own ears caught the note of reservation in my tone. It must be very obvious to someone as perceptive, as close to me, as Rusty. "Well, I'm not quite sure," I corrected. "It's so hard to tell from letters what a person really means, how he feels."

Rusty waited a moment, then asked, "You think he may be getting interested in someone else?"

"It's not that. Oh, he's dating, just as I've been when the opportunity arose. But nothing serious, nothing that would make any real difference between us. This is no outside influence. It's more subtle than that. His letters lately sound as if—well, as if he's taking our relationship more for granted than I want him to. He writes as though we're all set, as though there's no question about our getting engaged when I get home and, eventually, married."

"And you're not sure that's what you want?"

"I'm almost sure it is," I had to admit. Then, with a little embarrassed smile, "But I want to be—if you'll pardon an old-fashioned word—wooed first. I don't want it all taken for granted, as if there isn't any question about my feelings. On the other hand, maybe he's not doing that at all. It's so hard to tell from letters. The written word seems so much more—inflexible than the spoken one."

"I know," Rusty agreed. "When a man speaks to you, there's his look, his touch, the inflection of his voice, to make his words have different meanings. All of that's missing in a letter."

"You're telling me?" I sighed.

My glance fell to Brad's letters, lying there in my lap. Was I reading something into them that he didn't mean, getting into an emotional tizzy over nothing? After all, I supposed I should be grateful he continued to write so often, that absence hadn't made his heart grow fonder of someone else. If we could just have been together, face to face in the moonlight, or even across a table in the Student Union, I had a feeling he could have talked away my fears and questions in nothing flat. But here I was, thousands of miles from him. And months would elapse before we'd see each other.

"Don't worry." Rusty's hand was comforting on my shoulder. "Things will work out for you two. I feel it in my bones."

"Do you, Madame Fortune-teller?" My grin was a little crooked. "I hope you're right."

But somehow, at that moment, I was by no means sure she was. . . .

18

A NIGHT TO REMEMBER

While Rusty and I had been in Europe, two wonderful prospects had developed. Her parents were planning to fly over, meet us in Germany at the start of our spring vacation late in March and take us motoring with them. And mine were planning to sail over and pick us up when our school term was finished; then the four of us would travel for several weeks before going home together. Naturally we both grew more and more excited about all this, as letters flew back and forth and the details were worked out. But this didn't mean we weren't enjoying our day-to-day life and living each hour of it to the full, in the wonderful French way.

We settled down to classes seriously with the start of our second semester. We'd been lucky enough to get high grades so far, but things might be tougher from now on. I'd be taking French translation and lit at the Institute for Foreign Students, classical drama and social psychology at the University of Aix-Marseilles, and only philosophy, European lit and French grammar at the Institute for American Universities. And all my subjects except two would be taught in French. Moreover, I'd not only be kept busy with studying, but also with the legwork required to get from class to class, since the University was several blocks away from the two Institutes.

I was also taking one more subject, but it was such sheer fun, I hesitate to call it a study. Soon after our return from Austria, Joan and I made the intriguing discovery that there was an excellent riding academy on the outskirts of Aix. How its presence had escaped our notice so long, I can't imagine, but naturally we proceeded to go riding there our first free afternoon. The horses were quite spirited and the lean, athletic, middle-aged gentleman who ran the place was droll and charming. From him we learned that by taking lessons and riding twice a week we could get physical education credit from the Institute. And the cost would be only twenty-five dollars apiece for a whole semester.

How could we resist? It might mean I wouldn't have to take P.E. my senior year back in the United States. And even if this wasn't the case, I'd have the fun of riding regularly and of learning from a fine, experienced rider. Joan was as enthusiastic over the idea as I, so we decided then and there to sign up. Nor were we ever to regret it for a moment. Our association with Monsieur Jacques and the heavenly spring afternoons we spent on horseback are memories we'll always cherish.

My studies were a bit more difficult than they had been during the first semester, but I enjoyed the challenge they afforded. To listen to lectures in normal, rapid-fire French and grasp their meaning gave me a heady sense of accomplishment, as did my growing ease in speaking the language. Rusty, too, had grown much more fluent in our adopted tongue.

Although we were studying harder, there was still

plenty of time for fun. Rusty continued to spend most of her free evenings with Steve and it made me happy to see them so happy together. Looking ahead, though, I realized this was going to be a sort of hard spring for me, with no special man around. I was missing Brad more than ever. There was an empty ache inside of me that no amount of busy-ness and amusement could cure. As we wrote back and forth, his attitude toward our relationship was discussed and the attendant complications ironed out. Brad was perfectly willing to go through whatever romantic preliminaries I desired in our courtship. He just wanted to go on record that he still felt the same way about me as he had when I left—only more so. And he hoped I hadn't changed in my basic feeling toward him. Looking as deeply as I could into my own heart, it seemed to me that Brad was still the one. Nothing had happened to alter that—nothing, that was, which a few weeks of seeing each other again couldn't straighten out. But it was going to be such a long time before we saw each other!

One night Rusty came in from a date with Steve to fling herself down across her bed and exclaim disgustedly, "Men!"

"What's he done now?" I queried.

"Not he—they," Rusty corrected, her brown eyes flashing sparks of indignation. "Steve's pals have been working on him again. It took me all evening to convince him I wasn't just dating him because the competition doesn't amount to much."

"Old inferiority complex gnawing him again?" I sympathized. "I hope you did convince him."

"I think so," Rusty's sigh was dreamy. "If I had the

entire male portion of an American university to choose from, I'd still take Steve. But I hate to come right out and admit a thing like that. It might go to his head."

"He's pretty sensible," I said. "Why not risk it?"

"But then—what if I change my mind?" Rusty's voice was so low I had to lean closer to hear her.

"You think that might happen?" My heart ached a little for Steve at the very thought.

"It always has before," Rusty admitted. "I guess I am pretty fickle."

"But a girl can change," I said. "You have changed a lot this year, Rusty, in so many ways, just as I have."

"I know," she nodded. "But how can I tell if I've changed in that respect? I've never dated any one man as long and steadily as I have Steve—or felt the same way about any other one, either. But—everything's so different over here. How do I know what my feelings will be when I get home again?"

It was a question no outsider could answer; she'd have to work things out for herself. I merely reminded, "If Steve goes to a college in the States next year, as he hopes to, you'll have a chance to find out whether he seems as attractive in a more familiar environment."

"That's right," Rusty agreed, brightening. "I really don't have to work out every problem inherent in our relationship right now, do I?"

"Easy does it," I grinned at her. "Take them one at a time, that's the best way. Your psychiatrist has spoken."

But I couldn't help keeping my fingers crossed mentally for Steve. He was such a swell guy!

The quaintest sort of old-world carnival came to Aix in February. There were shooting booths and wheels of fortune, a carousel with tinkling music and a couple of rides similar to those found at American Legion and V. F. W. carnivals back home. Naturally the Institute kids flocked to it, and it seemed equally popular with the French, so there was a gay crowd milling about every night. The boys tried their skill at the shooting gallery and we ate strange confections and rode the rides and had a lovely time. The only trouble was, it left us all feeling homesick.

The carnival's final night fell on Mardi Gras. Fat Tuesday is a big occasion in France, we were to learn. All the lights in Aix were turned out by city authority Then the townspeople gathered near the Fountain of the Four Dolphins to watch an impressive display of fireworks flower into noisy brilliance against the ink-black sky. There was much excitement and friendly talk and laughter as everyone enjoyed to the full this big night of gayety before the start of Lent. We Americans found it reminiscent of Fourth of July celebrations at home.

Life in Aix was comparatively calm and quiet after that for a while. Then a situation developed which seemed so glamorously unreal as to be scarcely believable. One of the Institute students from Delaware, a girl named Cathy Gerard, was a good friend of a naval officer's wife back in her home town. This friend had written Cathy that her husband's ship was at harbor in Marseilles and that the young officers aboard were eager to meet the American girls they had heard were at school in the vicinity. She had asked Cathy if we might be interested in a sort of collective date with them. Cathy, in the supreme understatement of all time, had written back to say she didn't think we'd mind. So the upshot was that we received a formal invitation to dinner and a movie aboard the U.S.S. *Macon* the following Friday night.

The excitement around the Pavillon was indescribable. Thirteen of us girls planned to go and such hair washing and setting, such manicuring, such refurbishing of party clothes as went on you can't even imagine. I cut all four of my Friday classes, I made such a big production of getting ready. And Rusty was just as bad.

"Doesn't Steve care if you go?" I asked, as I eeled into my girdle for the first time in weeks. It seemed a bit tighter than usual. I'd have liked to think it had shrunk, but I feared it was all the rich French food I'd been eating.

"He gave me his blessing," Rusty smiled. "After all, this is one of those dream occasions that may only happen to a girl once in a lifetime. He didn't have the heart to object."

We went by bus to Marseilles, our excitement mounting with each mile. Our first sight of the great sleek ship was a thrilling one and the American flag flying against the clear blue sky brought a lump to our throats. Thirty young ensigns, handsome as gods in their natty uniforms, welcomed us aboard. There were some older officers around, as well as a crew of ordinary seamen, but we scarcely noticed these, so dazzled were we by our prospective dates—two for each of us, we calculated roughly!

We sat down to a delicious American-type dinner in the officers' mess. Unfortunately, due to the snugness of my girdle, I couldn't eat very much. But I enjoyed every mouthful I could manage. And between the enthusiastic attentions of Don on my right hand and Jerry on my left, I wouldn't have cared if a crust of bread was all they served us. Having gone manless so long, who cared about mundane things like food?

When the gracious meal was over, we were taken on a full-scale tour of the ship. This proved extremely interesting, especially with Jerry holding open every door for me and Don helping me up and down each step as though I were not only infinitely fragile and precious, but blind as well.

Next we settled into deep man-sized seats in the officers' lounge and saw a movie. It was quite old and not very good, but no one minded. Before the lights went up at the end of it, Don whispered an exciting invitation into my ear. The ensigns wanted to escort us back to Aix and take us dancing.

"All of you?" I asked, wondering what dance place in Aix could accommodate such a crowd, plus its usual patrons.

"No, no," Don said hastily. "We'll pair off—if that's okay with you?"

Of course, it was. After all, he'd asked me first. Besides, he was cuter than Jerry and several inches taller.

That was quite an evening! Rusty ended up with a dark-haired young officer named Bruce and Don and I sat facing them on our ride back to Aix. There were ten couples in all, a few of the girls having begged off for one reason or another. We danced at the Moulin d'Huile until far into the night. And Don and I got along just fine. He was from Wisconsin, I learned, and had a degree in chemical engineering from Northwestern.

He also had a nice wide grin, short-cut brown hair and a keen sense of humor. And he could dance. Naturally, when he asked me for another date the following Sunday, his first free time, I accepted with pleasure.

When Rusty and I were getting sleepily ready for bed, she told me that she'd made a date with Bruce for Sunday, too. "He and Don will come up together—maybe rent a car, so we can go driving in the country and have a picnic supper. Wouldn't you like that?"

"Of course," I said. "I love picnics." But then I couldn't help asking, "What about Steve, though?"

Rusty shrugged. "I'm going out with him tomorrow night—and, after all, he doesn't own me. Wasn't this all fun?"

"Terrific," I admitted.

But after we had talked about the evening for a while, I asked, although I knew it wasn't any of my business, "You don't really like Bruce as well as Steve, though—do you?"

"Of course not," Rusty said. "But variety is the spice of life and I've had darned little of it lately. Tonight sort of whetted my appetite."

She sounded like the gay casual character she had been when we first met, not the more mature person she had seemed to be developing into during our months in France. Somehow I didn't feel I knew this Rusty very well. It was almost as though a stranger were climbing into the bed next to mine.

Long after the lights were off and Rusty's even breathing indicated she slept, I lay there thinking, wondering how it was all going to turn out.

19

RUSTY MAKES UP HER MIND

Saturday night Rusty went out on her date with Steve and I took a long walk with Earl Bristol, the young man we'd met on shipboard and who had shared our initial mad pilgrimage across France. We had remained friends in a completely casual and undemanding way. Tonight we ended up at a sidewalk café, discussing, as usual, a wide variety of topics—conformity, which we both deplored, materialism, of which we were a little weary of hearing Americans accused, although there was certainly cause for the accusation, and French politics, which are quite difficult for any outsider to understand.

When I got back to the Pavillon, I was amazed to find Rusty there before me. She was creaming her face, but a suspicious pinkness about her eyes led me to wonder if she could possibly have been crying. Since Rusty wasn't addicted to tears, I had a strong urge to ask if anything was wrong. But not wanting to pry, I said merely, "You're back early."

"We had a fight," her tone was desolate and when she turned to face me, her lower lip trembled.

"I'm sorry. Was it—about tomorrow?"

She nodded. "He put his foot down. Last night, he said, was different—a big party, lots of people involved—but a real date was—well, more personal. And I said I had a perfect right to date anyone I chose to. And he—he agreed. He said quite calmly that that was true, that I had the right, but if I used it, we were through. Just—" she swallowed, "flat—like that—"

"Do you suppose he meant it?"

"I think so," Rusty said forlornly. "I never knew anyone like him before. He can be so firm, so—final. Every other man I've known, I could get around if I really wanted to. I—tried with Steve and it didn't work at all. He just listened calmly and then said it was up to me to decide whether we had something worth keeping, worth helping develop, or—or whether I just wanted to go on forever, flitting. Flitting," she repeated indignantly, "that was the exact word he used! No one ever talked like that to me before!" Suddenly her indignation seemed to ooze away. "So, I simply came in and left him standing out there in the courtyard and now—now I feel perfectly awful. Judy, what shall I do?"

"It sounds as if you've already done it," I said.

"What do you mean?"

"Decided you and Steve didn't have anything worth keeping. That's really the basic issue, isn't it? Unless that was the case, you surely wouldn't risk losing him just for the passing satisfaction of going out with someone else, who actually doesn't mean a darn to you. Or are you really interested in Bruce?"

"Of course not," Rusty denied. "But—I've never let a man order me around, tell me what I can or can't do—"

"Has Steve ever seemed dominating before, as if he wanted to do that?"

"No," Rusty shook her head slowly. "No, he hasn't. He's always been reasonable and thoughtful—and sweet —" She sounded as if she were going to say more, but she didn't and that last word sort of hung in the air between us for a long moment.

Then I asked gently, "Why don't you see how you feel about it all in the morning, when you've had time to think?"

"That would be a good idea—" Rusty sighed, "I guess."

I don't know whether it was sleeping on it that helped her to a decision in the matter, or whether the long talk she and Steve had the following morning turned the trick. Luckily Don phoned around noon to tell me what time he and Bruce could get to Aix. And Rusty talked with him and asked him to explain to Bruce that something had come up and she couldn't keep her date with him. She said she was sorry, but she certainly didn't look it. There was a positive glow about her and it was just as well her dreamy smile wasn't transmittible along tele phone wires.

"So Steve won," I teased, after I'd hung up.

"I think we've both won," Rusty answered softly.

I had a happy suspicion she was right . . .

Don wasn't able to get a car for that afternoon, but I really didn't care. I'd always loved walking and in Europe the habit had grown stronger than ever. I showed him Aix and introduced him to a crowd of my fellow students when we stopped at Les Deux Garçons for coffee. Later we had dinner at Aix' most elegant restaurant, where I hadn't eaten before. This was Don's idea, not mine, but I won't say I didn't enjoy it just as much as he did. We proved increasingly congenial and had even more fun than on our first date. And when, in parting, Don asked if he could come to see me again on Thursday, his next free time and the last night his ship would be in port, I agreed with pleasure.

Those next three days dragged a bit. It wasn't that Don and I were seriously interested. But even a few dates with an attractive man do something for a girl's morale. And, after all, it was spring, which comes early and beautifully to the south of France. So naturally I was grateful to fate for being so kind.

Thursday night we went dancing at the Hot Club, with Rusty and Steve and several other couples. This is quite a place, very popular with students of all nationalities. You enter by means of an extremely small door, similar to the bottom half of a Dutch door. Crouched down as you are, you're scarcely prepared for the steep flight of stairs that descends just inside. With Don's strong arm around me for support, we groped our way down through the half-darkness to a dim-lit cavelike basement room. An excellent combo was playing American jazz and the joint was really jumping! We were lucky to find a place to sit. Some of the tables were conventional ones, but others were big flat-topped rocks. And all the seats were real tree stumps. They weren't too comfortable to sit on, but no one sat much. We danced and danced and had a wonderful time, although I kept wishing Don were Brad. Maybe he wished I were someone else, too, some girl back in Wisconsin of whom he was terribly fond.

"What are you thinking about?" Don's voice was low.

But, of course, I wasn't going to tell him. "Just what a fun place this is," I smiled, "and how nice it is to be dancing."

His cheek pressed my hair. "You're telling me? I wish I didn't have to leave tomorrow."

"So do I, but let's not think about it now."

"Okay," Don agreed. "We'll pretend tonight's going to last forever."

I wasn't willing to go that far, but I didn't come right out and say so. No sense spoiling the fun. Later, when we were saying our good-byes in the moonlit courtyard of the Pavillon, I felt a very real sense of regret. It would have been wonderful to have Don around a while longer. Such a whirl as he had given me made life much more exciting. Why couldn't he have been a student at the Institute instead of an ensign in the navy? He couldn't have taken Brad's place permanently, but he would certainly have helped fill up the emptiness left by our being so far apart.

The next few weeks passed calmly, but swiftly. I found my second-semester classes more intriguing than my earlier ones, especially the course in psychopathology I was taking at the French University. This was utterly fascinating. And with the lovely spring weather, Joan and I enjoyed our riding lessons more and more. Our rides took us along winding dirt farm roads, through a half-rough-and-natural, half-cultivated countryside. Farmers plowing with their huge draft horses always greeted us in the friendliest fashion. And the warm sun shown down on the greening trees and shrubs and grass along the roadsides. Millions of blossoms in every pastel shade were bursting into fragrant bloom. And I'll never forget the time we came out of a shadowy spruce grove to see all of Provence spread out beneath us, with the towering peak of Ste. Victoire clearly visible in the distance.

Often a crowd of students rented bikes and rode out into the country for a picnic lunch on week-ends. Or we would sit for hours at a sidewalk café over a cup of chocolate or a pastry, talking and talking. The proprietors didn't mind this. In France no one seems to care how long you linger at a table. There is an air of leisureliness, a complete lack of hustle and bustle, that gets into the blood and slows down even the tourist who is simply passing through. What it did to all of us who were staying for ten whole months would probably affect us the rest of our lives.

Not that we didn't take advantage of all the available diversions. We saw a Russian movie which had won the Cannes Film Festival award, attended a performance by a touring opera company, heard a jazz concert. We played bridge and went dancing, half a dozen couples together, at the Hot Club or Moulin d'Huile. But if there was nothing special to do, it didn't bother us. Rusty and I could spend a wholly enjoyable evening just talking, or reading, or writing letters. The tension and frustration of our early weeks in Aix seemed quite incredible to us now.

Of course, we were looking forward to meeting her parents in Germany in March and traveling with them by car all during our spring vacation. Afterwards, the Stanleys would make Aix their headquarters for another week while they toured southern France.

"I'm so glad," Rusty said one evening when we were discussing their arrival, "that they'll get to meet Steve while they're here. He'll get back from visiting his folks about the same time we reach here."

I nodded, understanding her feeling exactly. When a girl grows as deeply attached to a man as Rusty had to Steve during the past few months, she is anxious to have her parents know and admire him as she does. I couldn't imagine that the Stanleys wouldn't heartily approve of Steve, still I could understand Rusty's eagerness to bring them together.

A week or so before the Stanleys were due to fly to Frankfurt, I walked into our room one Wednesday after my final class to find a wonderful surprise. Rusty had bought us a hot plate! This was something we had discussed more than once, but nothing constructive had been done about it until now. Of course, hot plates were forbidden at the Pavillon, since they used electricity and Madame frowned on this. But we knew of at least three others on our floor alone, so we couldn't feel too guilty about it.

The thing was, although the University cafeteria food was good and fairly varied, the University was several blocks from the Institute. We didn't mind this in the evening, but lunchtime was quite a scramble and we usually had to sprint to make our first class of the afternoon. And French students, we had learned the hard way, are allergic to standing in line. They push and shove and squeeze all their friends in ahead of you, all in perfect good nature, of course. Still, this tended to make our noontime meals something of a headache.

We had got into the habit of buying fruit and cheese

and crackers and not going to the cafeteria for lunch. But this wasn't very nourishing. And sometimes the aroma of cooking food from the other hot plates made our mouths water. Luckily Madame almost never came all the way up to the third floor and we knew our secret would be safe with Babette, the girl who cleaned our room and who was always on the side of the students in any controversy, since we were her contemporaries.

"Just think of the things we can fix now," I gloated. "Hamburgers, grilled cheese sandwiches, eggs, soup—"

"We can pop corn," Rusty put in when I paused for breath. "Steve brought loads of it from the P.X. last time he was home. Think of that and hot chocolate while we do our homework at night."

I was so thrilled with our new acquisition that I cut enormous letters out of cardboard and strung them up above our window to spell the word "*formidable.*" In French this means approximately "extraordinarily extraordinary." Rusty got a charge out of this, as did Babette when she first observed it. And when we gave her samples of some of the first goodies we cooked, her undying secrecy was assured.

Armed with one of those string bags we had seen so many Frenchwomen carrying to market, Rusty and I took turns shopping for delicacies of every sort. We would wend our way from shop to shop, buying meat in one, fresh, crusty bread in another, canned goods somewhere else and picking out vegetables and fruit at the outdoor market in the square. We ate cream of mushroom soup, hard-boiled eggs, cheeseburgers and packaged puddings made with powdered milk and sometimes combined with bananas to make fillings for graham cracker crust. And everything tasted delicious.

We resolved firmly to go on a diet a month or so before we were due to leave Aix, since we had each gained a few pounds. But in the meantime, we were really having a ball. One night we gave a popcorn party for a crowd of our friends. French and American girls assembled from all over the Pavillon. And Rusty banged away loudly on the typewriter to disguise the sound of the popping corn, just in case Madame should come snooping.

Of course we hid our hot plate carefully in a locked suitcase before we took off for Frankfurt to meet Rusty's parents. We didn't want to risk having it confiscated during our absence.

Every now and then, as our train sped toward Germany, Rusty would exclaim, "I just can't believe I'm going to see Mother and Dad so soon!"

The glow in her face indicated clearly how much she was looking forward to this meeting. I was looking forward to seeing the Stanleys again myself. I felt I knew them a great deal better since I'd lived with Rusty and heard her speak of them so often. In fact, I was anticipating their arrival with only a little less enthusiasm than if they had been relatives of mine.

20

BARCELONA, HERE WE COME

Those weeks at Easter time passed in a breath-taking blur of new places, new faces, new experiences. The Stanleys were charming traveling companions and their Mercedes ate up the miles greedily. We saw a great deal of Germany, the big modern cities like Munich and Stuttgart, the quaint Old-World villages nestling in the folded hills, where life seemed to go on in the slow, quiet pattern of an earlier time. We loved Heidelberg, with its moss-grown castle and ancient university. We stopped to explore art galleries and castles along our way and saw modern factories that reminded us of those in America. One could not but admire the energy and industry of the Germans in restoring their war-shattered country to some semblance of its former self. And the people were so friendly and cheerful, our contacts with them made it hard to remember that they had been our bitter enemies twice in the past half century. Or maybe it is better to forget.

We headed toward Paris, stopping overnight in the fairytale country of Luxembourg on the way. It seemed a perfect light-opera setting and one half expected to see peasant girls in full skirts and handsome uniformed guardsmen dancing on the green. Naughty Marietta or the Merry Widow would have felt quite at home there, I'm sure, although everyone we saw was dressed much like ourselves and no one seemed at all inclined to burst into song.

"Somehow," Rusty murmured wistfully, "I wish everyone didn't wear the same sort of clothes. It must have been much more picturesque in the old days, when each country was different."

Nodding, I couldn't have agreed more.

Paris was fabulous and we enjoyed every minute of our stay there. It has a special, heady atmosphere all its own, which is quite indescribable. You have to see it, feel it, taste it, breathe it with every breath. We tried not to miss anything. The Louvre, with its priceless art treasures. The Arc de Triomphe, beneath which the French unknown soldier lies at rest. Notre Dame Cathedral. Montmartre. The Sorbonne. We explored the Left Bank, where the stalls of artists and booksellers line the Seine. We window-shopped along the Champs Elysées and were awed by the beauty of the opera house. The Eiffel Tower proved disappointing by daylight. But at night, when it had changed miraculously into an airy outline of pure gold against the blue-black sky, its loveliness caught at one's throat. In fact, the whole of Paris is much more hauntingly beautiful by night than in the daytime.

I wrote Brad, "If you don't see Paris sometime, I can't bear it!" What I hoped, of course, was that we could see it together.

We turned our backs on Paris finally to drive south,

pausing at Versailles to see the magnificent palace of the French kings, then going on through the lovely château country that lies in the Loire River valley. This is some of the most beautiful scenery in all of France and we fell completely under the spell of its enchantment.

"But you know what?" I told Rusty as we were getting ready for bed our last night before reaching Aix. "I feel as if we're getting home. Does it seem that way to you, too?"

She nodded. "And I can't wait to show Aix to my parents! They've just got to love it the way we do."

"How could they help it?" I asked confidently.

The Stanleys' enthusiasm for Aix proved most gratifying and we had a wonderful time, displaying its many charms and points of interest to them. They lingered for almost a week, taking trips to Monaco and elsewhere on the Riviera. This gave them ample time to get acquainted with Steve. And, to Rusty's delight, they were quite favorably impressed with him.

"I felt they'd like him," she confided to me, "but sometimes parents' reactions are a little hard to predict. And he likes them, too. That's equally important."

"Yes, it is," I agreed, knowing how sunk I'd have been if my parents and Brad hadn't taken to each other at first sight.

With the Stanleys' departure, life settled into its calm routine once more. Studying and writing letters, horseback riding twice a week, frequent bridge games, occasional movies and the long fascinating talks that were such an integral part of student life. Sometimes we were quite profound, but, of course, we had our lighter moments, too, when we got pretty silly.

Rusty and I continued to enjoy our hot plate. One night we had a pancake party, although it took forever to make the pancakes, since we could only cook one at a time. But this merely served to whet our appetites. In April my parents sent me a food package and soon afterwards Rusty received one from her grandmother. We and our cronies gorged ourselves for days on peanut butter, marshmallow fluff, and all sorts of American type goodies.

"But we are positively going on a diet the first of May," we kept assuring each other.

"We should be able to lose five pounds apiece in six weeks quite easily," Rusty said firmly.

"Maybe we ought to make it six or seven pounds," I suggested. "Remember those meals on shipboard?"

I had no intention of getting back to Brad a single pound heavier than I had been when last I saw him. His letters kept dwelling on my gorgeous figure and attractive legs and I certainly wasn't going to disillusion him.

One day late in April, Rusty came into our room to exclaim, beaming, "Guess what Steve wants me to do!"

"Elope?" I kidded, knowing they were too sensible for that.

"Go back to Germany with him when school's over and meet his parents! He'll have his mother invite me, of course, but when she does, do you think we could possibly work it out?"

"Why not?" I asked. "Sounds to me like a great idea."

"But will it fit in with your folks' plans?" Rusty asked anxiously.

"Sure," I nodded. "They want to spend a few days in Aix and then drive leisurely over to the coast and up to Paris. If you went home with Steve, you could meet us there."

Rusty's eyes were shining. "I'd love to do it. I've wanted to meet the McConnells, hearing Steve speak of them so often."

His plans for studying next year in the United States were pretty well set by this time. He'd be going to Colorado, where his grandparents lived. So this seemed a made-to-order opportunity for Rusty to get acquainted with the McConnells. Knowing the increasing depth of her feeling for Steve, I could understand her eagerness.

A few days later she received a warm invitation from Steve's mother, which she accepted delightedly. And plans were made for her and Steve to leave Aix as soon as the school term ended. Thus Rusty could spend several days in Germany before joining us in Paris.

The warm days slipped away with almost incredible swiftness. We couldn't believe our stay in Aix was drawing to a close. Mom and Dad wrote that they were counting the days until they would sail from New York in mid-May, only a few weeks hence. I was looking forward to summer, to being with Brad again, with even greater enthusiasm. But at the same time I was clinging to each hour of these last days in Europe, steeping myself in the oldness of things, reveling in the slow pace of life. I wanted to soak it up, make it a part of my very being, so that I would never lose it, never forget.

One night I said to Rusty, "You know, time's running out and there's one place we wanted to see and never have."

Rusty nodded, looking up from her book. "Spain."

"Do you suppose we could possibly squeeze in just a short trip there?" my tone was wistful. "After all, we'll see Holland and Denmark and Sweden and some of England with my folks. And we've covered Italy and Switzerland and quite a lot of France. But Spain sounds so intriguing."

Rusty grinned. "Let's check on the possibilities."

We learned at American Express in Marseilles that we could fit a brief trip to Madrid, by way of Barcelona, into four or five days. The announcement by Mr. Maza a short while later that there would be no classes on the first Friday in May was all we needed to trigger our resolution. Our grades were high enough so that we were permitted unlimited cuts, provided, that was, the professors whose classes we cut weren't planning tests for that day. By leaving Wednesday morning and catching a noon train for Spain, we'd miss only two days' classes, added to our free Friday. And it would give us almost five days for travel.

We made our plans accordingly. But we were stopped cold by a sign on the bulletin board announcing a quiz in our Wednesday morning lit class. Consultation with Mr. Maza established the fact that we'd have to clear our cut with the professor in order not to be penalized for missing the quiz. This proved a problem, since the professor in question lived in Avignon and could not be reached by phone. And so, sadly, we just about gave up hope of getting away.

Still, the idea that maybe we could work things out kept nagging at us. We both wanted to go to Spain so badly. Tuesday night we sprawled across our beds, sipping our customary hot chocolate and regretting the necessity of wasting our free Friday entirely. We kicked around the possibility of taking a shorter trip, perhaps to somewhere we'd missed in Italy. After a lot of serious discussion, the thought of what we were doing suddenly struck us and we practically went into hysterics. Here we lay, late at night, not a preparation made, not a bag packed or a ticket bought, calmly considering taking off for one end of Europe or another the following morning.

"It's as if," I howled, "we were back home, with a Friday off from school, trying to make up our minds whether to leave the next day for New York or California!"

"Which only proves," Rusty laughed, "that we're changed women! So let's quit all this fiddle-faddle and pack."

"For Spain?" I wiped away my tears.

"Where else?" Rusty said. "We may never have another chance to see it."

We packed a small train-case apiece, hid our hot plate, and went to bed. Next morning we were up bright and early, rushing around the markets buying food for our lunch and dinner on the train. Rusty took our stuff to the bus station while I waited, poised and ready like a rocket on a launching pad, in front of the Institute. Our lit professor arrived at ten and immediately gave us permission to cut class and take the quiz later. I covered the six blocks to the station at such a sprint that the calm, slow-moving citizens of Aix watched me in open-mouthed amazement, then looked back curiously to see who might be pursuing me. But I didn't really mind.

It would only strengthen their conviction that all Americans are a little mad. And we caught the ten-fifteen bus.

"Barcelona, here we come," Rusty exulted as we boarded the noon train from Marseilles with all of five minutes to spare.

We fell panting into our seats and sat for a long moment, just grinning foolishly at each other. When I had caught my breath, I said, "It had better be good, after all this!" I still couldn't quite believe we had made it.

But, once more, we were riding along, train wheels clicking their accompaniment to our hopes of high adventure. And when Rusty and I went traveling, anything could happen and probably would!

21

GOOD-BYE, AIX

We ate our sack lunch, being more careful about quantities than we might have earlier, since we were now on our diet. We had just finished when two young French soldiers, quite dashing in their uniforms, entered our compartment and sat down facing us. They lost no time checking as to whether we spoke French. But we pretended not to, since they seemed pretty bold and we didn't want to get involved. It was hilarious, sitting there understanding them perfectly, but not letting on by so much as the twitch of a facial muscle. Especially since we seemed to be their main topic of conversation. After a while the heat and the motion of the train began to make us drowsy and Rusty fell asleep.

Soon one of the soldiers, with a childish grin, tore off a strip of his newspaper and began tickling her ankle to annoy her. I made signs of "No," to which he responded by starting to tickle my ankle instead. This soon got tiresome, so I finally looked him dead in the eye and asked in perfectly adequate French, "How old are you, Monsieur, twelve or thirteen?"

That settled him, but we were just as glad when the two soldiers left a few stations farther along. Their places were taken by much more congenial traveling companions, a Spanish boy of eighteen or so and a darling, middle-aged Spanish woman. They weren't together, but they began talking. And enough of my high school Spanish came back to me, coupled with the small amount of French and the few words of English they knew, so that we grew quite friendly. The woman told us all about her family, whom she loved dearly, and even fished a whole stack of pictures from her voluminous purse to show us how good-looking her husband and children were. Mothers, I guess, are the same the world over.

The boy, Jose, whose home was in Barcelona, assured us that it would be almost midnight before we reached that city. From there, he estimated it was another ten or eleven hours by train to Madrid. And connections, he added regretfully, weren't always good. We might have to wait hours.

"How about flying?" I asked.

"A matter of two hours at most," he beamed. Then his smile faded, "But one needs a reservation in advance —I think."

Jose proved invaluable in Barcelona. He found out for us in the station that there was no train to Madrid until the next morning. Then he got a taxi and insisted on going with us to the main airline's office. This was closed, with a sign on the door stating that business could be conducted at the baggage office in another part of town. The three of us went there, only to learn that the line's night plane and all its next day's flights were full. However, the helpful man at the desk suggested that we try the office of a different airline, which just might still have seats available on its night flight. Of course, all this information was in Spanish, which Jose passed on to us in his halting French. I don't know how we'd have got along without him!

Luckily the other airline office was open. And the attendant assured us there was ample space on their night flight. We couldn't understand why he seemed so delighted to see us. Later we were to learn that this particular line had recently suffered several bad accidents and that passengers were comparatively few and far between. But, all unknowing, we agreed when he told us we could ride out to the airport on their passenger bus.

We thanked Jose and said good-bye to him warmly. He wouldn't even let us pay for the cab we'd been riding around in. When we tried to press money on him, he just shook his head and smiled.

"Remember when you return home," he said in parting, "that chivalry is not dead in Spain."

How could we forget it after knowing him?

On our way out to the airport, a heavy fog settled in. Upon our arrival we were told that all flights had been cancelled due to bad weather. The next plane to Madrid wouldn't take off until eleven in the morning. And it was now only a little after one. Without a word of consultation, Rusty and I headed wearily for the airport waiting room. It looked quite comfortable and we weren't about to start back to the city in search of a hotel at this hour.

We took turns, one of us sleeping while the other

watched over our possessions. No one was going to get a passport away from us this trip. Sunshine pouring in the windows woke us. It was quite early, but we felt fine, all things considered, except for ravenous appetites. Over breakfast we decided to check with the first airline we had tried last night, in case they had had any cancellations on their early morning flight. And this time luck was on our side. There were two cancellations, which we immediately grabbed up. So we flew to Madrid on their choice flight, arriving at ten o'clock in the morning.

First of all we tried to locate an American girl named Linda, the fiancée of Earl Bristol. We had met her on shipboard, too, and Earl had given us her address. We found her apartment without much trouble, but she wasn't at home. So we went sight-seeing on our own. After all, our time was limited and we wanted to make the most of it. We inquired our way to the Prado, Madrid's famous art gallery, which proved almost as interesting as the Louvre and not nearly so crowded. We spent most of the day there, wandering about interestedly and even discovering a restaurant in the building that served, of all things, American hot dogs and something vaguely resembling ice cream sodas. Late in the afternoon, when we were about ready to leave the gallery, we happened on a crowd of students busily taking notes on a lecture by the Prado director. And there among them was Linda and also Dick Walters, another American we had met on shipboard coming over.

We fell on each other delightedly and, naturally, they cut the rest of the class and took us to a nearby sidewalk café, where we sat talking and drinking Pepsis. It is amazing how American food and soft drinks seem to turn up all over the world. Next Linda and Dick helped us find a nice inexpensive hotel and then Dick drove us all in his little snub-nosed Volkswagon out to the edge of the city to see the huge University of Madrid, with its beautiful campus and striking modern buildings.

Dick dropped us off at our hotel, to rest and get cleaned up. Later he and Linda took us for an extensive tour of the city by night. Rusty and I were starving, but the others assured us you couldn't get dinner in Spain until around ten o'clock. Eventually we went to a most interesting restaurant. Here we ate, by picking them up on toothpicks, delectable enormous mushrooms cooked in a rich meat sauce.

Madrid, both Linda and Dick assured us, is not really Spain. Its beauty and cleanliness, the wide streets, the well-designed modern buildings, the trees, grass and flowers growing so lushly wherever you look—these go to make up Franco's showplace for all the world to admire. But the true Spain is composed of mountains and jagged rocks, barren wasteland, tiny villages so poverty-stricken and filthy they aren't even picturesque.

We saw none of that side of Spain. The bus tour we took the following day was apparently carefully planned to give tourists the best possible impression. The countryside we traveled through was rocky, but ruggedly beautiful. And we enjoyed the time spent at El Escorial, a huge stone combination church and palace built for a Spanish king in the sixteenth century. It now houses a monastery and boys' school and there are many ancient hand-bound-and-printed books, works of art and interesting tapestries and religious relics.

In the afternoon we drove on to the Valle de los Caidos, or Valley of the Fallen. Here in a wild green gash surrounded by mountains, Franco had built a monument to those who died in the Spanish Civil War. There is a stone cross five hundred feet high and a church is built back into the rocky hill beneath it. The architecture is modern and beautiful and the whole thing most impressive, whatever one's feeling about Franco himself.

That night we again saw Linda and Dick and sat around talking until quite late. Saturday morning we walked about sight-seeing and window-shopping until time for our flight to Barcelona. We spent the night in a pleasant hotel in that busy industrial city, then caught a train early Sunday morning for Marseilles. Our trip back was uneventful and no one nearly as charming as Jose turned up to add interest to it.

"Isn't it funny," Rusty remarked when we were safely back at our room in the Pavillon, "to think of all the wonderful people we've met on our travels, whose paths we'll probably never cross again?"

I nodded in agreement and we sat silent for a time, as the long parade of them passed by in our thoughts. Pietro, with his shy smile. The little man in Florence, who had carried our suitcase and been so grateful for our company on his lonely Christmas day. The two American soldiers we had met on the commuter boat in Venice. The pleasant woman who had sent her daughter to lead us to St. Mark's Square. The Spanish mother showing us pictures of her family. And many, many more.

They had given us a much clearer, truer picture of

what the people of other countries were like than we had had when we came to Europe. Had we helped them to a better impression of Americans by our words, our actions? I hoped so.

Now our time left in France could be measured in weeks, rather than months. And, finally, only days remained. Once again there were good-byes to be said, addresses to be exchanged, promises to write given, which might or might not be kept. Mr. Maza made a small speech on our final day of classes. He hoped, he said, that we had found our year at the Institute a happy and rewarding one. He felt, he went on, that programs such as this and the many others offered, would help the young people of different countries to a better understanding of each other's lives and traditions and problems.

"And such understanding," he finished, "is in my estimation, the hope of the future."

The small "Amen" I added was no less forceful for not being said aloud.

On our last night together in Aix, Rusty and I went for a long walk. Tomorrow she and Steve would leave for Germany. In a day or so my parents, who had phoned me last week from Italy, would be here. And eagerly as we were both looking forward to the summer and to the time beyond it, there was a queer little feeling of loss in our hearts, at the realization that our year here was nearly over.

We didn't talk very much. Somehow words didn't seem necessary. Every narrow street, every familiar shop window, every sidewalk café with its brightly painted tables had something to say to us, something we might not hear if we didn't listen.

The leaves of the great plane trees arching above the Cours Mirabeau seemed to whisper softly, "Good-bye, good-bye," as the evening breeze stirred them. And the words were picked up in a more sprightly rhythm by the tinkling of the Fountain of the Four Dolphins.

Aix had given us so much—an appreciation of another, more leisurely way of life, the ability to take time to enjoy the present, to relax completely. Never again would I attach such world-shaking importance to a schedule; never would Rusty feel that each minute of the day must be filled with some activity. But Aix had done even more for us. Here we had been thrown into such close association that each of us had benefited richly by the differing aspects of the other's character. We hadn't discovered interests in common so much as our very personalities had grown to encompass the other's interests as well as her own. We were broader individuals, with more varying facets, because of our friendship. And this was good.

Never would we forget this ancient French town, or the experiences, some funny, some sad, but all interesting, that had been ours here. Neither would we leave without a sharp ache of regret for something sweet and young and irreplaceable that we would leave in these surroundings. Sometime we might return, but it wouldn't be the same—it couldn't! We wouldn't be twenty, or students, or in love with life and France.

The future beckoned us both and it wore a lovely face. We would answer its summons gladly. But not without a backward look, a last look at the ancient town dreaming under the stars, to which we had brought so much of hope and expectation and from which we would take with us infinitely more in the way of experience and wisdom.

I looked at Rusty and her eyes were suspiciously bright. Probably mine were, too. At least, I felt like crying. But instead, I asked, "Shall we get something to go with our hot chocolate later? After all, we've lost five pounds apiece on our diet."

"Let's," Rusty nodded vigorously. "How about those little round cookies that are usually still hot from the oven?"

"Why not?" I shrugged in the French fashion. "We'll live it up tonight."

And, arm in arm, we headed back toward the Pavillon.

In December after our return home from Europe, Rusty and Steve were married. And the following summer I married Brad. So this true story has as happy an ending as any work of fiction. Or even more so!

Judy du Jardin